A MESSAGE FROM CHICKEN HOUSE

H is Royal Hopeless has a wicked fairy-tale queen at its heart – but her heir and our hero, Robbie, is a great disappointment: friendly, optimistic, clumsy and clueless . . . you'll love him! He sets out on an epic quest to prove he's worthy of his evil inheritance, but a firm friendship, a few knockabout accidents and a lot of determination are about to turn his evil aspirations upside down. Can he learn to embrace who he really is? Chloë Perrin's debut story turns a fairy tale on its head, and then, once firmly dizzy, she sticks it on again back to front. Laugh-out-loud, wise and the best fun!

BARRY CUNNINGHAM
Publisher
Chicken House

HIS ROYAL HOPELESS

CHLOË PERRIN

Chicken House

2 PALMER STREET, FROME,
SOMERSET BA11 1DS

Text © Chloë Perrin 2021
Illustrations © George Ermos 2021

First published in Great Britain in 2021
Chicken House
2 Palmer Street
Frome, Somerset BA11 1DS
United Kingdom
www.chickenhousebooks.com

Chicken House/Scholastic Ireland, 89E Lagan Road, Dublin Industrial Estate,
Glasnevin, Dublin D11 HP5F, Republic of Ireland

Cover and interior design by Steve Wells
Typeset by Dorchester Typesetting Group Ltd
Printed and bound in Great Britain by CPI Group (UK) Ltd, Croydon, CR0 4YY

1 3 5 7 9 10 8 6 4 2

British Library Cataloguing in Publication data available.

ISBN 978-1-913322-30-4
eISBN 978-1-913696-12-2

For FS.
Robbie would be even more lost without you.

A Sinistevil come of age
May step before the Sceptre's glow
And pledge their heart of flesh and blood
Which then with hate shall overflow.

Heed this warning, Kings and Queens,
Who seek to kill the Sceptre's heir;
Those who obstruct the course of power,
Their wicked life shall not be spared.

CHAPTER ONE

In the centre of Waning lay a castle, a castle of dark brick and twisted turrets which leant over its kingdom as though about to take a bite out of it. Within this castle of terrified servants and endless cobwebbed corridors lay a bedroom, a bedroom with a family tree painted meticulously down one wall.

The name on the tree was known throughout the kingdom of Waning – largely because it was the name of the rulers who kept burning down people's houses. It was a name that could silence a room, that could make a cavalry run for the hills, that could send shivers down even the sturdiest of spines. The name was that of their rulers, of the most despicable, distasteful and downright *evil* royal family in the entire world.

That name was written in bold, spiky silver letters, painted stylishly and with exquisite care at the top of the family tree. The name read:

The Sinistevils

The royal family tree was a gnarled one, a *nasty* one. Sinistevils did not play nice with one another, and most family gatherings ended with a few more branches snapped off. Even so, it was a tree that thrived.

Near the bottom of the tree, in angry violet lettering, was the current ruler and matriarch of the Sinistevil household: Queen Viella Sinistevil, who liked to crush peasants and laugh as their villages burnt. The silver line of the tree wound down to her equally cruel eldest son, the late Prince Brutus, who led the armies and laughed equally hard at the burning of villages.

However, Brutus was not the final name on the tree. Right at the bottom, crammed up against the skirting board, was another name. The people of Waning had not yet seen Viella's surviving son and heir to the throne, whose name on the tree was obscured by a crowd of lint and dust-bunnies. But they *did* know his name. The boy who could only be as vile and disgusting as the rest of his bloodline, who could only be as evil as evil can be, was called . . .

'Ahhh-*choo*!'

Robbie Sinistevil woke with a sneeze and sat up in bed, drawing a long pyjama sleeve across his nose. 'Good morning!' he said to the silvery tree snaking across his bedroom wall, as he hopped from under the covers.

As Robbie threw open the curtains on what was promising to be an absolutely glorious morning he assumed, like the rest of the kingdom did, that he was as evil as evil could possibly be. Why would he ever think otherwise? Robbie was a Sinistevil, and Sinistevils were evil. Evil was his legacy. It was in his blood. It was in his – he looked at his sleeve and grimaced.

Time to get dressed.

Robbie pulled his robes out of the wardrobe. They were black, of course – the only acceptable colour for a Sinistevil to wear – and suited him perfectly.

Well, maybe *perfectly* wasn't quite the right word: they didn't actually *fit*. The sleeves of the cloak fell past Robbie's hands and further still, while the bottom of his trouser legs pooled around the soles of his shoes. But that didn't matter to Robbie. Sleeves could be rolled up, trousers could be hemmed (or stapled; Robbie was not skilled at sewing). What mattered was not how the clothes *looked*, but what they *represented*; they'd been his brother's.

Robbie turned back to his family tree and dropped to his knees, smiling at the emerald name *Brutus*. 'See you in a bit!' he said with a wave. He then rose without realizing he was standing on the corner of his cloak, tripped forwards and hit his head against the bed post, where it gave a resounding *bonk*. Robbie rubbed his pointy nose and smiled bashfully at Brutus' name. 'I'm sure you did that all the time,' he said brightly.

You see, there was a pitfall in the assumption that the youngest Sinistevil was the evillest being known to man. This was the fact that when it came to being pure evil, Robbie Sinistevil . . .

Well, *wasn't*.

*

Robbie skipped out of the door and began the journey down the winding corridors of Sinistevil Castle which would eventually, with any luck, end in breakfast. The sound of his oversized boots pounding the flagstones of the castle floor echoed down the empty corridors, softening as they hit the deep red carpet of the portrait wing. He passed painting after painting of green-skinned ancestors, some glowering down from glorious battle scenes, others simply glowering down.

Robbie stopped at the fifteenth portrait to the left, stepping on to the worn patch of carpet in front of it. He looked up and sighed, taking in his favourite painting.

It was the goriest painting in the castle and, quite possibly – although Robbie could not know this – the goriest painting in the world. Vivid reds and purples depicted limbs scattered across a battlefield, some still attached to people. Sinistevil warriors shook nasty-looking weapons at weeping villagers, weapons that seemed cruel, unusual and altogether quite frightening.

Robbie liked the picture. He was *sure* he liked it. If he tried hard enough, he could even look at it for more than a few seconds before his stomach protested. It was definitely creative; Robbie hadn't known blood could come in so many different shades of red, and the expression of the man looking for his right arm was exceedingly emotive. Yes, it didn't matter if Robbie felt queasy in its presence; if this was indeed the goriest picture in the castle, then Robbie decided that he must like it, because he was evil and evil people like gory things.

However, this was not the reason Robbie considered this painting his *favourite* painting in the castle. The reason it was his favourite was because it had his brother in it. There he was, in the upper left corner, grinning with childlike glee as he set a nearby peasant alight.

Now *that* was a Sinistevil.

There were lots of paintings of Brutus Sinistevil in the castle, he even had his own gallery in the south wing, but in Robbie's opinion none of those paintings depicted Brutus nearly as dynamically as this one. Robbie puffed up his skinny chest with pride as he gazed up at his big brother, who held a burning torch in one hand and the green jewelled Sceptre glowing in the other. So strong, so villainous, so powerful. And Robbie thought it only fitting that the best painting of Brutus in the whole castle showed him doing what he loved: levelling innocent villages.

Brutus represented a benchmark for all young Sinistevil heirs, heirs such as Robbie himself. If he stared hard enough at pictures of Brutus, Robbie could even convince himself that he shared a lot of his brother's features. It wasn't that Robbie considered himself attractive (he knew he wasn't – Mother had told him so); it was that, genetically speaking, he was made up of all the things every other Sinistevil was made up of. His skin was the green of congealed algae, his warm yellow eyes ringed with deep grey. Like his brother's, his hair was thick and black as an oil spill on a reef. Unlike his brother's, it stuck out rather more than it should.

The only things missing were the muscles, which Brutus seemed to have an excess of. Some days, Robbie secretly wished Brutus had left some for him; by the time *he* was eleven, Brutus' arms had looked like overfilled potato sacks, while Robbie's currently looked like damp noodles. He'd only been one year old when Brutus had died, but Mother assured him Brutus had always come home from battle looking like the dead returned to wreak revenge, whereas Mother had once described Robbie's short, wiry frame as that of a bemused scarecrow.

Robbie wasn't worried. He was optimistic – a trait he had inherited from no one, but seemed to have developed all on his own. It was due to this inexplicable optimism that Robbie was certain he would fill out his late brother's clothes by the time he turned twelve. He would *have* to, or else he wouldn't have the strength to wield the Sceptre when he pledged his heart. He looked back to the Sceptre painted in Brutus' hand, the glow it emitted bathing the surrounding gore in a soft green. Every Sinistevil had been bathed in that mesmerizing glow, and some day soon it would be Robbie's turn . . .

The thought of the Sceptre made Robbie's stomach gurgle, and he decided that now was the time for breakfast.

After all, it was irresponsible to be evil on an empty stomach.

CHAPTER TWO

Robbie did not live alone in Sinistevil Castle. There were the staff, of course, but there was also *someone else*. Someone who stalked the hallways like an irritated storm cloud on a breeze of disgust.

This creature also bared the trademark Sinistevil features, but more so. Her teeth were black and ragged, and her fingernails resembled her teeth. Her body was like that of a tarantula: squat and haggard, yet still able to move with incredible speed. Her face rarely smiled, and when it did you had reason to be frightened.

This person threw open the dining hall doors,

sending them crashing into the walls with a force that knocked over two candelabras and half a dozen servants. Robbie looked up from his breakfast and smiled.

'Oh, good morning, Mother.'

Mother sneered at Robbie from the other side of the table, her yellowy-white eyes rolling upwards with contempt. 'How can it be good?' she snarled. '*You're* here.'

Robbie chuckled; how he enjoyed Mother's sense of humour in the morning. He went about eating his toast, unaware of the eyes training themselves on his every move from across the table. Robbie lifted another slice to his lips.

'Look at you,' said Mother. 'What are you eating? *Toast.* Chewing away like a lousy little insect.'

Robbie swallowed his mouthful. 'If I don't chew, I could choke . . .'

'And what a day that'll be!' spat Mother. 'I'll throw a parade!'

'Wow,' said Robbie, smiling as he reached for his orange juice. 'I'd get a parade all for me? I've barely done anything.'

There was a low rumble from Mother's throat.

The servants exchanged anxious glances, and a particularly pale-faced one hastily disappeared from the room. It was no secret that Mother despised Robbie with a burning hatred so intense you could roast marshmallows on it, a hatred made all the more vibrant and dangerous when faced with Robbie's interminable cheeriness. The servants were well aware of the patterns Mother's verbal jabs usually took when it came to Robbie, and knew that in a moment she was going to bring up her favourite subject: the comparison of brothers.

'Idiot!' she said. 'If your brother were here, there would be none of this *juice* and *toast* – it would be hog roast for breakfast, and that cup would be filled with the blood of his enemies!'

Flecks of green spit rained on the tablecloth as Mother continued her tirade. Robbie listened with his chin in his hand. 'Woooow,' he said dreamily. 'What else would he have for breakfast?'

'*Idiot!*' Mother banged her fist, sending mugs jangling across the table.

The pale-faced servant reappeared and discreetly dropped something in front of Mother. The castle staff also knew the only way to calm Mother's dining room tirades was with the arrival of the morning paper.

Mother snatched up the paper in her talons and held her greasy nose up to the front page. Her chapped lips curled into a grin. '*Sinistevil Army Quells Rebellion with Extreme Violence.* What a wonderful headline.'

'Can I see the cartoons?' called Robbie. Mother tore the back page from the paper and chucked it over the maroon tablecloth. Robbie caught it as it fluttered down in front of him. 'Did Brutus ever read the cartoons?' he said as he straightened out the crumpled paper.

'He read the financial section,' replied Mother through gritted teeth. 'Because he had a *brain*. Hm,' Mother drummed her fingernails on the table, 'this is a similar headline to yesterday's paper.' Her head snapped up as she locked gazes with a terrified servant, whose legs began to shake under Mother's scrutiny. 'If this isn't today's paper, the one who's responsible will have their tongue pulled out through their ears – and you know that's not a mere threat, because you've seen the painting of the procedure in the portrait wing.'

'Why don't you check the date?' said Robbie from behind the cartoons.

'I don't need advice from a toady little juice-swilling worm like yourself!' spat Mother as she scanned the top of the front page for the date.

If Robbie hadn't been so preoccupied with the cartoons section, he may have noticed Mother's face changing, its usual green becoming tinted with a sickly mottled pink. He would have noticed her yellow eyes widening and her mouth slowly twisting to reveal those jagged black teeth.

As it was, Robbie was so engrossed that he didn't even notice Mother had got up until she'd snatched the page from his hands, scrunched it up and thrown it at his head. She was already at the dining-hall doors when she turned and said, 'I'm no longer in the mood for breakfast. Looking at your face has ruined my appetite.'

'Oh,' said Robbie. 'Well, I do hope you feel better soon.'

'*IDIOT!*' Mother screeched, and she slammed the door behind her.

The servants breathed a collective sigh of relief as Mother's footsteps disappeared down the corridor.

As they set about clearing the table, Robbie pondered what he was going to do with the rest of the day. He didn't want to stay around the castle, especially if his face was making Mother ill – what if they ran into each other and it worsened her condition? He wouldn't be able to live with himself if that happened.

One of the servants brushed against the dining hall's thick purple curtains, and a sliver of light caught Robbie's eye. The curtains were always drawn in the dining hall because Mother detested so much as a hint of sunlight, and Robbie had forgotten what a beautiful day it was. What time was it? If it was still early enough, he could visit his friend.

Of course, Robbie noted, that involved *sneaking out*. Robbie did not take such things lightly; as prince and heir to a throne hated by the entire kingdom, leaving the castle walls was an extremely difficult and dangerous task. He could be murdered by the townsfolk – that is, if he was lucky enough to get past the extremely vigilant castle guards. However, Robbie was not new to the concept of sneaking out, and knew exactly how to do it. All he needed to do was slip past the servants and disappear without anyone noticing.

As inconspicuously as he could manage, Robbie pushed back his chair and strolled out of the room, closing the door carefully behind him.

'Where's he off to, do you think?' said one of the servants.

'Oh,' said another. 'He's probably sneaking out to see that friend of his.'

'Aw,' said the first servant. 'That's nice.'

CHAPTER THREE

It is common knowledge amongst parents, teachers and most locksmiths that the term 'impenetrable fortress' means nothing to small children, who seem to be able to get everywhere regardless of how hard a person tries to keep them in one place.

The Queen considered the Sinistevil fortress to be utterly impenetrable, and for the most part it was. What she *didn't* know was that if a small child of around six were to drop the coin they were playing with in the east wing, they would then follow it. If the shiny object were to roll away down some stone steps and up to a particularly grizzly tapestry of

Lazarule Sinistevil inventing the game Kick the Bear Head, that small child might come across a draughty, crumbling piece of wall with a hole just big enough for a child of around six to fit through, a hole which led to a passageway. That child may then emerge from a tunnel directly behind the hovel-like home of one Layla Granite, also aged six.

Robbie had been sneaking past Mother to see Layla ever since. With practice, he had managed to get quite good at it.

The castle staff also knew about this tunnel, mostly because they had found Robbie stuck in the hole numerous times. However, they had collectively decided *not* to inform the Queen of the tunnel or Robbie's friend. This was due to the fact that they had never known a Sinistevil to be capable of something so innocent as friendship, which to them made Robbie's excursions to Layla curious, intriguing and absolutely adorable.

Robbie emerged into the morning sunlight on his knees, scrabbling through dirt until he reached the familiar brown grass of Layla's village. He brought himself to his feet, tripping on his baggy trouser leg as he crept across the grass to the truffle tree that stood behind Layla's shack. His skinny frame was hidden by the thick trunk as he reached for the lowest branch and tugged it, making the leaves bob up and down one, two, three times. Then he waited.

'Took you long enough.'

Robbie jumped, then spun around excitedly to see his friend. Layla grinned as she brushed the tight black curls from her deep brown forehead. While Robbie's smile was broad and goofy, Layla's grin was bold, toothy, and dangerous – the kind of grin that said you were either about to be hugged or punched.

Robbie could never help but return this grin, but after a moment, he frowned. 'Wait – were you expecting me?'

Layla crossed her arms and sat down heavily against the trunk of the tree. 'Of course – I *always* know when you're about to appear in my yard, Robbie Sinistevil. I can smell the clean. Come on, sit down, my parents are at the market.'

Robbie slid down next to her. 'Isn't it a lovely day?'

Layla snorted. 'Every day's a lovely day when you live in a castle and don't have to work for a living. I've been digging up potatoes since six a.m. Look at you,

you're ninety per cent soap, whereas *I* have my own dust cloud.'

Robbie nodded. 'I hear mud is good for your skin.'

Layla flicked at the encrusted dirt on her overalls. 'Then my skin has transcended goodness.'

'Are those new overalls?' said Robbie.

Layla smiled and her face glowed with pride. 'Yes, made them myself! Another potato sack tore yesterday, so I got a whole new outfit.'

Layla posed, showing off her patchwork overalls, which were made up of patches of anything and everything she could get her hands on. Brown sack, purple linen, even the tartan of an old quilt cover. If someone else had discarded it, you could be certain Layla would stitch it together and add it to her wardrobe.

'I don't know what potato sacks are,' said Robbie. 'But they look lovely on you.'

'You pampered little rich boy,' said Layla, shaking her head.

'I'm not pampered,' said Robbie. 'I am a finely tuned war machine.'

'I'd like to see that.'

'It's true! One day I'm going to pledge my heart to the Sceptre, receive its power and lead the Sinistevil army, and I'll do it all with the Sinistevil iron-barbed fist.'

To illustrate his point, Robbie made a fist. It was a very thin, angular fist. Layla prodded it gently, making Robbie hiss.

'Ow! Not so rough!'

'You're so weak! You're like a sentient pillow.'

'I am not. I am a vicious tiger.'

Layla laughed and pushed Robbie's shoulder. Despite it being the lightest of pushes, Robbie's lack of anything close to balance sent him sprawling to the ground.

'I'm fine,' said Robbie, spitting out dirt.

'I hope pledging your heart will be easier than this!' Layla snorted as she reached out a hand. Robbie laughed too, but once he'd sat up he noticed Layla's smile wavering.

'What's the matter?' he asked as he brushed the soil off his cloak.

'What will it be like, do you know?' said Layla, her voice a little hushed. 'When you pledge your heart to the Sceptre?'

Robbie's face lit up. He cleared his throat and puffed out his chest as he recited:

'*A Sinistevil come of age*
May step before the Sceptre's glow
And pledge their heart of flesh and blood
Which then with hate shall overflow.'

He grinned smugly at Layla, who frowned back at him. 'That was lovely,' she said. 'Good projection, wonderful diction. But what does it *mean*?'

'I read it in one of my great-great-great-great-aunt's diaries! Mother gave it me to read.' Robbie beamed proudly. 'To shut me up because I kept asking questions. They're ancient instructions, passed down from Sinistevil to Sinistevil! That's what it's going to be like when I turn twelve and can finally pledge my heart to the Sceptre.'

'*Hate shall overflow?*' said Layla, her voice unsure. 'Doesn't exactly sound pleasant.'

'Power isn't always pleasant, Layla,' said Robbie, folding his arms. 'It's a cross we Sinistevils have to bear.'

Layla rolled her eyes. 'I'm so sorry for you.'

'But I do agree,' said Robbie. 'The instructions are a bit vague – the diary ended awfully abruptly for some reason, before she'd even explained anything. Either way, I'm certain it'll all become perfectly clear when I come of age and finally get to go into the Sceptre Room and see the Sceptre for myself. Maybe there'll be more instructions on the—'

'Wait, wait, wait,' said Layla, holding up her hands. 'You've not even *seen* the Sceptre before?'

'Of course not,' said Robbie indignantly. 'It's an extremely important Sinistevil artefact! In fact, the last person to even hold the Sceptre was Brutus.'

'I didn't know Brutus pledged his heart to the Sceptre,' said Layla. 'Doesn't that mean he was King?'

'Oh, yes,' said Robbie, nodding so enthusiastically his bushy hair fell into his eyes. 'He became King just before he died in battle.'

'Not a long reign, then.'

'About half an hour, Mother said. Either way, Brutus was the last person to hold the Sceptre, which is probably why Mother doesn't want me touching it before I've come of age.' Robbie gasped as a thought occurred to him. 'It might still have his fingerprints on it!'

'If that's the case,' said Layla, 'then I'm sure your

mother has it displayed in some sort of shrine.'

Robbie leant back against the tree. 'Imagine if it has his hand-print on it – I could see if our hands were the same size!' He stretched out his hand in front of him and sighed. To hold the Sceptre that Brutus himself pledged his heart to! He couldn't turn twelve soon enough. Then he thought back to breakfast and scratched his chin. 'She was in a funny mood today, Mother.'

'What do you mean?' said Layla. 'Was she nice to you? Did she give you a hug?'

Robbie blinked one of his patented slow blinks, which gave his mind time to catch up with the words he'd just heard. 'I don't know what you mean. She's *always* nice to me. And she never hugs me because she doesn't want to catch diseases.'

Layla frowned. 'Catch diseases?'

'Well, she said something about not wanting incompetence to rub off on her, and I can only assume that's some kind of disease, so I respect her wishes.'

Layla sighed.

Robbie could never understand why Layla felt the way she did about Mother. She'd never been anything but a wonderfully kind and affectionate mother to him, despite some of the things she regularly said about his intelligence and physical appearance. Perhaps Layla just didn't understand the concept of tough love.

'By the way,' said Layla, reaching into her pocket, 'I've got to go and meet Dad at the market soon, so I'd better give you this now. Happy birthday.'

In her hand she held something small, flat and crumbly, like a cake someone had accidentally stepped on. In fact, the more Robbie looked at it, the more he was convinced it was exactly that. His eyes started to glisten as he took the gift from Layla's hand, holding it together in his spindly fingers. It was . . . beautiful.

Then he looked up. 'This is a cake, right?'

Layla huffed and looked away bashfully. 'Yes, of course it's a cake. A birthday cake! Don't look at me like that, I'm good at clothes, not cakes. Besides, I had to hide it in my pocket so my parents wouldn't see it.'

'But it's not my birthday . . .' said Robbie, '. . . is it?'

'Yes, it's your birthday,' said Layla incredulously. 'June the eighteenth, same as every year. You're not telling me you forgot, are you?'

'I just didn't know today was the eighteenth.' Robbie put the cake into the pocket of his robe, looking up in time to catch another of Layla's eye rolls. 'Well, it's not like it's a special occasion, is it?' said Robbie. 'Why would anyone want to celebrate *me*?'

Layla crossed her arms. 'Oh, of course, I forgot that your loving mother doesn't celebrate your birthday.'

Robbie sighed. 'Well, you can't expect a working mother to have time set aside to celebrate her child's birthday, it's just not feasible. She has neither the time nor the effort to spare on such things.'

'Except for your brother, whose birthday is a national holiday.'

'Aha!' Robbie raised his index finger. 'But his *death* day isn't! Therefore, Mother is probably waiting for me to die before she ... celebrates ...'

Layla opened her mouth to scold him, but then stopped. Robbie had taken the cake out of his pocket again, and was turning it over in his hands with an expression of such dopey joy. He looked up at Layla with that big, goofy grin and said, 'I love it.'

Layla smiled widely. 'I'm glad.'

Robbie slipped the cake back into his pocket – then gave a jolt as his insides all lurched at once. He leapt to his feet.

'Wait a minute,' he said. 'Today's my birthday. That makes me twelve!'

Layla stood up and frowned. 'Sure,' she said. 'What's the big deal with twelve?'

Robbie tried to come up with the words, to voice the possibilities, but his brain wouldn't slow down enough for him to *think*. He began to pace, immediately tripping on his trouser leg and whacking his head against a low-hanging branch.

'Ow,' he said.

'You know,' said Layla, watching Robbie rub his head, 'I've got some thread left over. Are you sure you still don't want me to fix up your clothes?'

Robbie gasped. 'Of *course* I still don't want you to fix them!' He stood up straight and rolled up his cavernous sleeves. 'What would Brutus say if he knew I'd been stitching away at his perfectly fine royal cloak?'

'I think he'd have a thing or two to say about those staples in the legs. Now look, I've really got to go and help my parents, but have a happy birthday, okay?'

'Thank you!' said Robbie. 'And you have a happy ... potatoes at the market ... day.'

The two hugged, then Layla smiled and saluted before running back to her shack to grab her wheelbarrow. Robbie waved until she was gone, then turned to the tunnel. He had a rather urgent matter he needed to discuss with Mother as soon as possible.

CHAPTER FOUR

The rats of Sinistevil Castle resembled most things within the castle walls, in that they were much bigger and scarier than they really should have been. The same went for the spiders, flies, even the woodlice, all of which could normally be found scuttling about the castle halls, stealing food and terrorizing the servants. However, on this particular morning the rats were sticking to the dungeons and the spiders cowering in crevices. Anything that was able to was staying out of the hallways so as not to be caught under the deadly heels of the bigger beast storming through the castle.

The Queen was on the move.

The Queen of Sinistevil Castle was currently snarling her way through the halls, her iron-heeled boots making welts in the floor as she stomped up the corridors. This vision was made all the more terrifying by the fact that she was *smiling*.

Of course, the Queen was also a little nervous. There was a lot riding on this day, and a lot that could go wrong and spoil her perfectly laid plans. But if everything went correctly – if her plans succeeded – well . . .

Her terrible grin widened.

The Queen's talon-nails tore the wallpaper at every corner with a loud *THRIP*, warning the servants, who scattered like mice from an oncoming cat. She was still able to catch a few of the slower ones, who she picked up and hurled against the wall as she passed. Thank goodness the date on the newspaper had reminded her! She'd lost track of time, what with all the pillaging and village-burning she'd been doing lately. Never mind. It was finally *time*.

The Queen rounded a corner, checked for servants, then let her smile drop. Her high-speed march became an uneasy stroll as she turned into a hallway lined with suits of armour, where glinting, battle-worn helmets towered above her.

Now, now, she told herself, *there's no need to be anxious. The plan is fool-proof* – Robbie-*proof, even.* All she had to do was remind the little twit it was his birthday, perhaps even take him to the Sceptre Room herself. After that, the boy only had to put two and two together and try to pledge his heart – and all *she* had to do was make sure she didn't say anything to make him suspicious.

She caught her reflection in a suit of armour and stopped for a moment to straighten her cloak. But what if the boy *did* get suspicious?

The Queen's jaw clenched, her black teeth grinding as a growl rose up her chest towards her throat. She sent the suit of armour crashing to the floor as she began racing down the corridors once again, trying and failing to keep that horrible thought out of her horrible brain: the thought that if the little slug started asking annoying questions her whole plan would go straight down the drain. She knew what he was like; he was *incessant*.

The Queen inhaled deeply, her chest swelling like a toad about to croak.

'*DEVON!!*'

From somewhere in the castle came the sound of scuttling feet, growing louder and louder until the scrawny figure of Devon popped up from a nearby doorway. The perpetually terrified head servant flung up her hand in salute before noticing the Queen's trajectory: she was heading towards the gigantic doors of the grand Sceptre Room.

'*Open the doors!*' screamed the Queen, and Devon leapt into action. In a flurry of flailing limbs she sprinted ahead and strained every muscle in her body to push open the floor-to-ceiling double doors, just in time for the Queen to barrel through them. Devon panted as she wiped the sweat-slicked chestnut hair from her tawny freckled face. Being the youngest ever head servant at twelve years old may have been an achievement in any other castle, but at Sinistevil Castle it only made Devon feel that much closer to a heart attack. She tried not to think about this as she followed the Queen into the Sceptre Room, leaving the doors open behind her.

Devon had never been in the Sceptre Room before. It was even worse than she'd imagined it would be. The room itself was cavernous. Portraits and tapestries were draped across every wall, but were difficult to see due to the deep red velvet curtains blocking out every inch of daylight. Even the light from the hallway struggled to reach into the shadows of the Sceptre Room. The curtains soaked up sound as much as light, and with the Queen's footsteps on the white marble floor dampened, the room was plunged into an eerie, underwater quiet.

The one source of light inside the room came from its centrepiece, the most prized possession of the entire Sinistevil dynasty. On a golden pedestal, emitting a faint greenish glow and a low monotonous hum, lay the Sceptre. The soft glow of its bright green jewel crept across every wall of the Sceptre Room, as well as up the long narrow tapestry suspended directly above it, which rippled gently with the air currents of the room.

The Queen stopped in front of the pedestal, her hands floating above the treasure it held. She could feel the power flowing through the Sceptre, the power that was currently hers and hers alone. Its glow was brighter than usual, the hum louder. This was a good sign: it meant that the Sceptre was ready for a new owner. The Queen licked her lips.

'Devon!' she squawked.

Devon shuffled closer, her hands clasped so firmly behind her back they were almost white.

'Yes, my mistress?' she squeaked.

'Do you know what this is?'

Devon leant to peer past the Queen, and gazed at the glowing Sceptre. The ornate silver rod was patterned with deep black vines, culminating in the green jewel at the top. The heart-sized stone conjured images in Devon's head, both beautiful and nightmarish. She tried to ignore the sheen of nervous sweat she could feel on her forehead.

'That is the Sceptre, my mistress.' Devon's throat was dry; she didn't like being near the Sceptre, almost as much as she didn't like being near the Queen.

The Queen turned her attention back to the Sceptre. 'The Sinistevil bloodline is long, our empire vast. You know why this is?'

'Um . . .' said Devon, screwing her eyes shut. 'Hard work and determination?'

'Pah!' spat the Queen, and Devon instinctively ducked. 'No! It's because of *this*.' She ran her hand over the Sceptre. At her touch it let out a long hum which shook the very shadows around them. In a low voice, the Queen read from the tapestry hanging above them:

'*A Sinistevil come of age*
May step before the Sceptre's glow
And pledge their heart of flesh and blood
Which then with hate shall overflow.'

When the Queen spoke again it was in a hush, her raspy voice quivering. 'All Sinistevils are born wicked ... but to be as powerful as we are? That takes something extra. Even the wickedest of ordinary people suffer from inconvenient pangs of –' the Queen gagged, '– *conscience*. That is why my ancestor, the great and most gloriously vile Abomina Sinistevil, created the ultimate prize – something that would obliterate the very last shreds of goodness in her heart in order to harness, to *amplify* her evil ...' The Queen's lips curled into a smile. 'Within the Sceptre lies the source of unlimited darkness and power. Whoever wields it is capable of unspeakable things.'

Devon swallowed. 'Unspeakable?'

'A hate so thick it destroys your conscience, breaking every inhibition. Makes causing pain and sorrow so deliciously *easy*.' The Queen sniggered. 'And let's not forget, of course, the fear it instils in all others.'

'Yes, I've noticed that,' whispered Devon.

'Pustula Sinistevil –' the Queen stalked across the room, gesturing emphatically to a series of portraits which lined the wall, '– poisoned the wells of her enemies for fun. Tiberius Sinistevil, wiped out an entire species of fish because he was bored. Lavina Sinistevil, invented a weapon so effective that even saying its name causes blisters on the tongue. All exceptionally cruel creatures, all even crueller with the Sceptre.'

The Queen stopped in front of an enormous portrait of an exceedingly muscly young man. 'Oh, my dear sweet Brutus,' she wailed, raising her arms in despair. 'Oh, cruel fates! Why must you be so harsh? Why couldn't Brutus have been an only child? Why couldn't it have been Robbie to die in battle . . .? Huh. *Robbie* in *battle*. Can you imagine?'

She turned to Devon and grabbed the front of her bright red uniform, pulling her unbearably close. Devon could feel the hot stench of the Queen's breath against her nose. 'It's the little cockroach's twelfth birthday today,' she hissed against Devon's freckled cheeks. 'So we must be sure to get him in here to pledge his heart as soon as possible.'

'Excuse me, my mistress,' said Devon, trying to turn away from the smell. 'I'm so very, very sorry, but is that to say that you *want* the young master to continue the Sinistevil reign?'

'*Of course not!*' shrieked the Queen, flecks of green spit catching Devon in the eye. She wheeled around, flinging Devon halfway across the room as she did. 'Can you imagine Robbie ruling *my* evil kingdom? The miserable little weasel would run it into the ground! What I want is for the useless waste of space to be out of the picture for good – which is exactly *why* the boy needs to pledge his heart . . . or try, at least.'

Devon furrowed her brow, opened her mouth, closed it, then opened it again. 'My deepest apologies once again, my mistress,' she squeaked. 'But I'm still not sure I understand. If you *don't* want Robbie to ascend to the throne, why must we have him pledge his heart?' Her mouth snapped shut upon a look from the Queen. The corners of her lips curled into a cruel smile as her eyes moved towards the hanging tapestry above the Sceptre. 'You remember the little runt's *condition*?'

Devon thought for a moment, then followed the Queen's eyes to the words on the tapestry. *And pledge their heart of . . .* Her eyes widened in understanding. 'Yes, of course, my mistress,' she said. 'When Robbie was a baby and you – acting with impeccable grace and wisdom, of course – had his heart replaced with clockwork. He doesn't *have* a heart of flesh and blood.'

'The boy still believes he had life-saving heart surgery,' the Queen sniggered. 'Idiot. I would have dropped him off a bridge as a baby if those *finicky* little *time-wasting* rules had allowed it.'

'If I may ask, my mistress,' said Devon carefully, 'what will happen? When he pledges his clockwork heart?'

The smile on the Queen's face made Devon's stomach turn. 'Well,' she said slimily, 'let's just say the Sceptre takes its rules *very* seriously. I'll never have to worry about that little worm coming near my throne ever again.' The Queen snapped her fingers. 'Devon, the time has come. No more waiting. You are to find the snivelling little slug and bring him here at once. I will take care of the rest.'

Devon's eyes flickered back to the hanging

tapestry. She gulped. If Robbie tried to pledge his clockwork heart, she was pretty sure he'd die. But what could she do? 'Yes, my mistress.'

'Finally!' said the Queen, wheeling around with her hands outstretched, her face a picture of sheer horrific joy. 'After twelve long years, it will be bye-bye Robbie for *GOOD*!' She laughed a screeching laugh, and the glow of the Sceptre suddenly ebbed.

Her smile vanished. She spun around and gripped the corners of the pedestal, her eyes wide with panic. 'It doesn't count,' she said to the Sceptre, pointing a crooked finger at the tapestry above it. 'It doesn't count if he does it himself! I won't be to blame!'

The Sceptre did nothing in response. This seemed to calm the Queen, at least, and she turned on her heels and stormed towards the Sceptre Room doors, Devon skipping to her side. 'Stupid little rules,' the Queen growled under her breath, before turning to Devon. 'Go, fetch the little slug boy, and under no circumstance is he to learn of his clock-work heart. And if *anyone* lets slip our little secret, I will personally boil them alive in their own blood!'

'Yes, my mistress,' said Devon, panting as she jogged to keep up. 'Of course, my mistress.'

The doors were still open, but the Queen didn't walk through them. In fact, she stopped walking completely. When Devon caught up, she realized why.

'I don't suppose the Sceptre Room is soundproof, my mistress?'

The Queen didn't reply. She was too busy staring at the person who'd been waiting in the doorway.

'I have a clockwork heart?'

Chapter Five

It was a good few minutes before Mother was able to speak again.

At first everyone had simply stared at each other: Mother at Robbie, Robbie at Mother, Devon at the doorway, her exit, which was *oh so close*. Then Mother experienced the speechlessness only pure unadulterated rage could bring. Robbie didn't know quite how to process what he was seeing – Mother had just turned red, redder than anything he'd ever seen before, then deep purple, all in complete, unnerving silence. He wanted to offer her a glass of water, but was too afraid that if he moved, she might explode.

When Mother finally spoke, it was to quietly order Robbie to wait out in the hallway, which he did with pleasure, while she and Devon disappeared back into the Sceptre Room.

Robbie enjoyed being told to sit and wait. He was very good at it; it was one of the few things Mother said he was able to do correctly, other than being an idiot. It also gave him time to think, which was actually proving quite difficult considering all the racket that was coming from the Sceptre Room. He didn't know what was going on in there, but it certainly seemed loud.

At least Mother had her voice back. Robbie smiled. All was well.

Except . . . what he'd just heard . . . what Mother and Devon had been speaking about . . .

No. He must have misheard it. He'd think about that later.

Eventually, the door reopened and out shot Devon, so fast that Robbie didn't even get a chance to say hello. He liked Devon. She was very polite.

A shadow passed over him, and Robbie looked up into the yellow eyes of Mother.

'Hello, Mother,' he said brightly.

'Stand up, Robbie.'

Robbie got to his feet as Mother turned towards the Sceptre Room. 'Come with me.'

Robbie stood before the looming double doors and took a deep breath. This was it, he was finally allowed into the Sceptre Room. This was where his reign would begin, he could feel it. Now if only he could stop his hands from shaking . . .

'*HURRY UP.*'

Robbie tripped on his shoes as he shot through the doorway, hitching up his cloak as he jogged behind Mother.

The great double doors clanked shut behind him, taking with them the light of the hallway. He wasn't expecting to have to squint to see in the middle of the day. He supposed the unbearable darkness made the room . . . cosy. In its own way. However, it brightened towards the centre, where something lay emitting a green glow that bounced off the walls around him. Robbie squinted some more to see, but couldn't make out much apart from a sort of pedestal.

His eyes were then drawn to something moving above the pedestal, and he noticed the tapestry, which was still waving from the air currents of the doors slamming. The green glow illuminated it like an underwater light, and Robbie immediately recognized the verse it proclaimed:

A Sinistevil come of age
May step before the Sceptre's glow
And pledge their heart of flesh and blood ...

Heart of flesh and blood. Robbie felt something prod at his stomach. But Mother and Devon had said ...

No. No, that couldn't be right. Surely it wasn't even possible.

Suddenly the green glow brightened and Robbie heard a low hum reverberate about the room, a hum that brought a strange tightness to his chest.

'Ahem.'

Robbie quickly turned to Mother, and the glow ebbed. Mother was glaring. 'How much did you hear?'

'From yours and Devon's conversation?' said Robbie, finding himself automatically keeping his voice low. Mother narrowed her eyes and Robbie felt his skin crawl. 'Um ... there *was* something, a little snippet of a sentence before I could stop listening...'

'Yes?' Mother's eyes became even narrower.

'It was something –' Robbie chewed his lip, '– something that, if it were true – and I'm not saying it is, because it sounds pretty ridiculous – but if it *were* true, I think may pose an obstacle to me taking the throne.'

'And what was that?' said Mother darkly.

'That I don't have a heart of flesh and blood,' Robbie chuckled. 'Which of course, now I say it out loud, I realize *can't* be true, because that would mean I couldn't pledge my heart to the Sceptre.'

There was a spark in Mother's eye. 'You don't think it's true?' she said. 'So, you still want to pledge your heart?'

Robbie nodded hard. 'Yes, Mother, more than anything in the world.'

A wry grin spread across Mother's lips. 'How wonderful,' she said in a slimy voice as she extended an arm to the golden pedestal. 'Well, *I'm* not stopping you.'

Robbie gasped, then clasped his hands to his mouth. This was it, this was the moment he'd been training for his entire life. And Mother was smiling, just how he'd always imagined it! It was perfect.

But even through the pure sunshine pouring through Robbie's mind, he could still see a rain cloud lurking in the distance. He dropped his hands to his side.

'But if what you and Devon said about my heart *was* true . . .'

'Yes?' snapped Mother, lurching forwards so quickly Robbie nearly tripped backwards on his cloak.

'If – if . . .' he stuttered, 'well, it's just that in the diary you gave me, and – and the other books – well, they're all really quite adamant about obeying the Sceptre's rules, and if I'm somehow breaking them, then pledging my heart could . . .' Robbie looked into Mother's expectant yellow eyes, watched her shoulders hunch higher and higher with impatience, and suddenly all the words of doubt fell from his mind.

This was not a moment to be hesitant. This was a moment to make Mother proud. He turned slowly towards the golden pedestal and stepped closer to the green glow. The glow grew brighter and there was the low hum once again.

There it lay, right in front of him: the Sceptre. It

looked exactly as it did in all the paintings, except bigger and somehow more . . . solid. Robbie bit his lip and took a deep, calming breath. Of course, he *knew* he must have misheard Mother and Devon. There was no way on earth that he didn't have a heart of flesh and blood.

Unless . . .

Robbie's feet stuck to the floor as he lifted a bony hand to his chest.

'Well?' said Mother, her sharp voice cutting through the quiet like a bullet. 'What are you waiting for?' She began tapping the toe of her steel boots on the marble floor, making an awful *clank, clank, clank.* The noise did nothing to soothe Robbie's nerves, and he couldn't ignore it any longer. He sighed and turned back to Mother.

'I'm awfully sorry to ask,' he said, 'but when I was a baby, and you were so kind and gracious as to allow me to have that open-heart surgery . . .'

'What of it?' spat Mother.

'Y-yes, well,' said Robbie, wavering, 'I can't help wondering . . . see, I really would feel silly if this impacted my ability to pledge my heart, so . . .' Robbie swallowed hard as a vein in Mother's forehead looked ready to burst. '*Is* there something wrong with my heart?'

The room darkened slightly as the green glow dimmed. Mother glanced over Robbie's shoulder and a look of despair flashed across her face, a look that then melted into rage, which quickly dissipated into plain old disgust. She glared at Robbie.

'So, you won't pledge your heart, then?'

Robbie shuffled his shoes. 'I just feel that it would be better for me to know all the facts, purely so I can lead your evil empire in the best possible fashion.' He looked up with nervous eyes. 'I'd really hate to let you down, Mother.'

Mother sighed deeply.

'Well, I can't *make* you pledge your heart, *can* I?' She shot a glare at the Sceptre, which pulsed once in response. Mother redirected her glare at Robbie. 'You're leaving me with no choice but to tell the truth,' she hissed. 'And I *hate* telling the truth.'

'I'm awfully sorry, Mother,' said Robbie.

Mother scowled. 'What you heard was correct. You don't have a heart.'

All of Robbie's features began to droop ever so slowly downwards, like a snowman taking its time to melt. First his chin dropped so his mouth bobbed open, revealing the bottom row of his clean white teeth. Then his eyebrows fell to an expression of mild confusion, slowly working their way to complete and utter bewilderment. After what seemed an appropriate length of time, Robbie tried his hand at speaking again.

'I really *don't* have a heart?'

'No.'

'You mean in the metaphorical sense? Like, I don't have a heart for tyrannical leadership?'

'No, I mean in the literal sense. The squashy organ that pumps goo throughout your useless excuse for a body is not present.'

Robbie mulled over this idea for a moment. There was something about the situation that didn't seem quite right to him.

'I don't have a heart . . .' he said, '. . . and we're still talking about the organ?'

'Yes!' snapped Mother. 'You miserable little bag of half-bitten toenails! How is it that a boy your age can not understand this obscenely simple concept? You don't have a heart! You have a fake one, *obviously*. A little clockwork thing with cogs and springs or something – I don't know, I wasn't paying attention when they put it in.'

'Wow,' said Robbie. 'What a coincidence, to need open-heart surgery as a baby, only to have my heart removed later . . .'

'Do you even understand the mere concept of a *lie*?' Mother's voice oozed contempt. 'You didn't have *two* surgeries, you little idiot, you had *one*, which was to remove your heart and replace it with a clockwork one. And that is the last I will hear of it.'

And with that, Mother turned and stormed away. Robbie stood for a moment, staring at the spot where she'd been, before spinning round after her, struggling to keep up as his shoes slid across the marble floor. Mother was already halfway to the double doors before she realized Robbie was next to her, so she sped up.

'Mother,' Robbie called after her. 'Mother, please, I just – I just have one or two more questions, if it's okay to ask them.'

'It isn't,' said Mother.

'I understand that this must be a difficult topic for you to discuss – your son not having a heart and all,' said Robbie, starting to pant. 'It really . . . must be . . . quite traumatic for you . . . but I just have some teensy, very very little questions that I'd really like . . .'

Mother turned around, her body solid and hunched like an angry tombstone. Robbie skidded to a stop and took a few cautious steps back, tripping on his trouser leg and nearly taking a portrait off the wall before he regained his balance.

'Um,' he said, twiddling his fingers as he searched for the words. 'Well, firstly . . . if my heart isn't one of flesh and blood, like the tapestry says, how will I be able to pledge it? I don't know what might happen if I don't follow the Sceptre's rules to the letter – pledging it could – well, it could kill me!'

'*That was the idea.*'

'What was that, Mother?'

'Shut up!'

Mother stopped and looked up at the wall. Robbie followed her gaze and sighed. There, towering above them, was the most enormous portrait of Brutus he had ever seen in his life. He thought he'd seen all the portraits of Brutus that were littered throughout the castle – he made a pilgrimage to them every other day, purely to bask in his brother's glory – but he'd never seen anything of this scale. The room's green glow coupled with the sheer size of the painting magnified Brutus' massive, terrifying features; his biceps like sacks of boulders, a sneer that could make a starving lion turn vegetarian. Robbie gasped as he noticed Brutus was even wearing the very same cloak that Robbie was at that very moment. He bunched up the loose sleeves in his fists, noticing once again just how much the cloak hung from him.

The portrait only served to point out how small Robbie was in every respect, not just his clothes but his entire self. How minuscule. How absolutely, utterly *tiny*. Robbie had never felt quite so small in his life.

Mother stretched out a hand and gestured towards the portrait.

'Tell me, Robbie,' she said. 'How can you tell that your brother Brutus was the true born leader of an evil army of darkness?'

'Um . . .' said Robbie, thinking hard as he scrutinized the portrait. 'He's very tall, I suppose.'

'Look at his biceps!' cried Mother. 'The sword that can barely hold together in his iron grip! Look at his victims as they crawl away in fear! The blood on his armour, none of it his! The darkness that radiates from his very being!' She turned to Robbie. 'Now tell me, Robbie. How many of these features do you see in yourself?'

Robbie looked down, noting his wiry, stick-figure body, his big clumsy hands that would drop a sword as soon as wield it. How was he like his brother . . .?

'We have similar-shaped fingernails . . .'

'You are nothing!' said Mother. 'How do you expect to lead an army, to conquer entire continents?'

'I'd do my best for you, Mother,' said Robbie. 'No matter how weak and feeble I am, I would always do my best for you. I'm very determined. And I'm sure I could grow muscles if I really tried, and what I lack in physical strength I more than make up for in . . . brainy-type . . . strength . . .'

'You may want to *do your best*,' sneered Mother, leaning her face so close to Robbie's that her nose touched his. 'But *I* don't want you on my throne. So, I took precautions.'

Mother glanced behind her to the golden pedestal. Robbie followed her gaze to the tapestry, which was still swaying gently above it. He read past the first verse, the verse he knew by heart, to the second. This one he didn't know quite as well; memorization had never been his strong suit, and he'd aimed to have it learnt by the time he turned twelve. He sighed and read the verse, wishing he'd paid more attention to his calendar.

Heed this warning, Kings and Queens,
Who seek to kill the Sceptre's heir;
Those who obstruct the course of power,
Their wicked life shall not be spared.

Mother watched Robbie's pupils darting left to right as his mouth moved with the words. She rolled her eyes. 'You read so slowly.' She drew her long black tongue across her teeth. '*Those who obstruct the course of power.* An extremely *irritating* clause. Obviously, it meant I couldn't just kill you. So, I found a loophole.' Mother grinned, her teeth appearing like a set of knives. 'You were a baby when I had the idea. One of those tiny creatures, the disgusting kind that cough on everything and are always sticky. With your father having passed away...'

'I thought you killed him?'

'*HE WAS WEAK. DON'T INTERRUPT ME.* Anyway, I was the sole ruler of Waning and your glorious brother Brutus was my successor. Then he died in battle,' Mother paused to wipe a solitary tear from her cheek, 'plummeting from a castle balcony. And the only one left was *you*. Obviously, this simply would not do, so I went to the best doctorcerer...'

'Octowhaterer?'

'*Doctorcerer*, it is a doctor-sorcerer, and the next time you interrupt me I will rip your tongue out and feed it to my crows!'

'Sorry, Mother, it was incredibly rude of me, please carry on.'

'*Anyway*, the good doctorcerer opened up your little rib cage, tore out your heart and dropped in a different one. Anything would do, as long as it wasn't "*flesh and blood*". I recommended she sew your mouth shut while she was at it.' Mother rolled her eyes again. 'But apparently that was "a bit much".'

Robbie's brain was processing as fast as it could. 'So... I can't pledge my heart at all?'

'No,' sneered Mother. 'You *can't*. If it's not flesh and blood, you'll die. Get it now?'

Robbie shook his head. 'But there has to be some way! I know you must be worried about me trying to ascend the throne, what with my lack of muscles and brainy strength and everything, but if I could just prove to you that I'm capable . . .'

'*NO!*' Mother's voice made Robbie's back snap upright. 'There is absolutely *no way* for you to ascend the throne, so stop looking for ways to do it. I have worked too hard to keep you from ruining my empire, and I am not going to let you do it now just because you've found out a few little truths about yourself. I never want to hear you mentioning the words "pledge" or "heart" ever again, do you understand, you pitiful little worm child?'

'Yes, I understand,' said Robbie, but Mother was already walking through the Sceptre Room doors. He was left alone, standing under the sneer of his deceased brother, while the Sceptre hummed softly behind him.

CHAPTER SIX

The hallways of Sinistevil Castle were oppressively quiet, like a town that can't quite believe the hurricane is over, and dares not go outside to check. The staff were hiding in corners and behind tapestries; they'd heard about Mother's tirade, and no one wanted to be caught in the aftermath.

Robbie didn't notice that the castle was eerily void of other people. In fact, he hadn't noticed much at all since his news. He'd been sitting in the parlour for some time now, warmed by the crackling fireplace as he gently prodded the same spot on his chest over and over and over.

He felt . . . well, he wasn't quite sure *how* he felt about his news. Not really sad, more . . . surprised. Maybe a little conflicted; his initial reaction was that he should be panicking, distraught even, but Mother had given him the news so calmly that all those other reactions seemed a bit melodramatic now.

Still . . .

Robbie sighed. Maybe *confusion* was the correct name for the emotion, or at least for one of the emotions he was feeling. He opened his palm and placed it on his chest. Now that he was paying attention for the first time, he could feel it – the *tick-tick, tick-tick* of a clockwork pacemaker. *Well,* thought Robbie, *at least it seems to be working all right.*

But that wasn't the point.

The point was that he was finally of age to pledge his heart, and he didn't even have a heart to pledge. He wasn't able to rule. Everything that he'd been preparing for, everything that he'd based his life on, everything that was going to make Mother proud to call him her son, was gone.

How could he continue to call himself a Sinistevil?

Robbie looked up at the sound of the parlour

door creaking open. A small, nervous face peered around the corner, before darting away as it spied Robbie on the large leather couch.

'Devon?' called Robbie.

Devon's freckled face reappeared like an anxious moon emerging from the clouds.

'My apologies, young master,' she squeaked. 'I thought it might have been the Queen . . . though please don't tell her I said that. You're obviously deep in thought, I'll leave you be. I'm terribly sorry for the intrusion . . .'

'No, it's okay, you can come in,' said Robbie. 'In fact, to be honest,' he looked down at his chest, 'I think I'd quite like the company. Just for a bit.'

Devon hesitated. Being asked to keep a Sinistevil company was uncharted territory. She tiptoed into the room, her shoes making no sound as she shuffled across the black wooden floorboards. She stopped once she reached the couch, and awaited her next orders.

'You can sit, you know.' Robbie jumped as Devon recoiled at the suggestion. 'Are you all right?' said Robbie.

'My apologies, young master,' said Devon. 'It's just

that – well, it's – you see – if the Queen catches me sitting next to you then she'll cut off my toes and feed them to her crows, and that's not just a threat, because I've seen her do it . . .'

'I understand,' said Robbie. He looked down at his lap, then back up at Devon, a weak smile just about clinging to his face. The twitch at the corner of his mouth seemed to melt something in Devon, and Robbie watched as her face twisted in a moment of agonizing indecision. Then, slowly and carefully, she sat down next to him on the couch.

'I like your uniform,' said Robbie. 'Is the red to symbolize blood?'

'Yes,' said Devon, her voice just above a whisper. 'And the satin is for royalty.'

'It looks like a marching band uniform.'

'Yes, it does.'

'I have no heart, you know.'

Devon nodded. 'That's quite unfortunate.'

'See,' said Robbie. 'I knew it wasn't something to get all dramatic over. No one seems surprised about my lack of internal organs. I mean, *I* was, but that's not the point. I suppose lots of people don't have hearts. I knew I was being ridiculous.'

Devon swallowed. 'Actually, young master, I wasn't surprised, because . . . well, I already knew about it. I assure you, I was much more surprised when I first heard the news.'

Robbie blinked another long, slow blink. 'You knew?' he said. 'I suppose Mother told you.'

'Well,' Devon's cheeks began to grow spots of deep pink, 'actually, it was my father who told me. He was the previous head servant, you see, knew a lot about magic, and when Mother told him what she wanted to do he organized the trip . . . I'm very sorry, young master, it's awfully rude of me to talk about my personal life.'

'No, it's okay,' said Robbie. 'I'm sorry I've never asked you before.'

Devon looked guiltily at her feet. 'Truth be told, I think my father regrets the whole ordeal, he might even have wanted to tell you about your heart himself. He certainly sounded regretful when he told me, I suspect that's why the Queen had him put away . . .' Her back straightened and she bit her lip hard. 'Please don't tell the Queen I said that – obviously I suspect nothing of her actions other than impeccable wisdom and foresight.'

'Of course,' said Robbie. 'She's a very wise and foresightful ruler.'

For a moment they both sat in quiet and listened to the crackle of the fireplace.

'Mother told me I'd had open-heart surgery,' said Robbie in a small voice. 'I suppose it wasn't really a lie.'

Devon looked up at Robbie.

'I'm awfully sorry, young master. Are you all right?'

Robbie wasn't looking at anything any more. Everything around him appeared as an unfocused blur. When he spoke, his voice didn't feel quite connected to his body.

'I think so. You see, Devon, I have a bit of a problem now. If I can't pledge my heart to the Sceptre, there's no way of me becoming the ruler of the Sinistevil household. I'm not going to be able to lead armies to violently quell uprisings, or turn villages to ash, or any of the things that Brutus did.' *None of the things that would make Mother proud either*, thought Robbie as he fiddled with his dangling shirt sleeves.

'That is quite a predicament, to be sure,' said Devon, shuffling her feet.

Robbie stared into the fireplace again before sighing. 'It's just so frustrating,' he said. 'Being one of the most evil beings on earth and Mother *still* worrying about me pledging my heart. What else can I do?' He turned to Devon with pleading eyes. 'How can I show Mother that I'm ready for the responsibility? How can I show her how completely and utterly evil I am?'

Devon stared at Robbie, unblinking, for what felt like minutes. Eventually she cleared her throat. 'Well, of course I understand that you are a Sinistevil, and Sinistevils are incredibly evil . . .' She squirmed under Robbie's patient gaze while she tried to figure out the correct words to say next. 'I myself have always found you . . . your demeanour strikes me as somewhat . . . are you certain you *want* to rule the Sinistevil household? Not that you wouldn't be good at it,' she added hastily. 'You'd be an awesome, terrifying ruler, of course, but it couldn't hurt to . . . look at other options?' She gestured vaguely.

'Thank you for your honesty, Devon,' said Robbie, and Devon raised her eyebrows optimistically. 'It means a lot to hear you call me terrifying, it's exactly what I needed.' He sighed, and so did Devon. 'But I understand your hesitation,' said Robbie. 'I suppose I have been slacking.'

A sudden flash of determination lit up his face.

'Which only means that I must try harder! I'll be more like Brutus! Maybe tomorrow I *won't* have toast for breakfast, maybe I'll have . . .' Robbie thought furiously. '*Unbuttered* toast! With – with grapefruit juice instead of orange juice! That kind of looks like blood! Maybe when Mother sees all that she'll know just how capable I am of taking over her evil empire! And then it won't be long at all until I ascend the throne, wielding the Sceptre . . .' Robbie's smile disappeared. He sank back into the couch like a balloon with a leak. 'Except that I'll never be able to wield the Sceptre. Not without a heart of flesh and blood.' He sighed deeply and leant his head in the direction of Devon. 'I don't suppose you have any suggestions? Mother said that I shouldn't even *try* and find a way to pledge my heart because there was absolutely no point.'

Devon nodded sympathetically. 'There are certainly very few ways to return a heart, of course—' The

SMACK of her hands hitting her mouth reverberated off the parlour walls.

Robbie lifted his head. His mind slowly started to whir, like a carousel warming up.

'You mean to say,' he said slowly, 'That there *could* be a way to put my heart back into my body?'

'Nmph,' said Devon, before forcibly removing her hands from her face. 'No, young master, not at all . . .'

'And once my heart's back in my body,' said Robbie, 'I can pledge it to the Sceptre! All I have to do is get my heart back and I'm sorted!'

'Now, master!' Devon leapt to her feet with a look of wild panic. 'You really must not try to do that! The Queen has forbidden it! And besides, the Sunken Mountains are so very dangerous, you'd never make it to Dr Clampit's in one piece . . .'

'Doctorcerer Clampit lives in the Sunken Mountains, eh?' said Robbie, rubbing his chin. 'And you're certain of this? It couldn't be another doctorcerer, could it?'

Devon's lip quivered. 'That is the one that my father told the Queen to see, yes, but I can't in any way guarantee that they'll still have your heart! It's been twelve years – it might not even be in the same place Father saw them put it – and I don't know an awful lot about magical organ preservation, but ...'

'Magical organ preservation?' Robbie's eyes widened. 'So, it's entirely possible?'

'Oh no,' murmured Devon. 'Oh no, oh no, oh no, oh no, oh ...'

'You know,' Robbie began to tap his oversized boot against the floor. 'The Sunken Mountains are only a few days' walk through Bleak Forest. If I took the Sceptre with me, I could pledge my heart then and there – I could be King by next week!'

'*Please*, young master!' wailed Devon. 'Please, think about your *mother*!'

Robbie frowned. 'That's right – Mother! She told me not to go looking for a way to pledge my heart ...' Robbie stared into the fire for a moment, the light of the yellow flames flickering off his green face as he chewed his lip. Then he stood up. 'Well, of *course* she didn't tell me about the destination of my heart. She knows that Bleak Forest and the Sunken Mountains are incredibly dangerous places – if she's already worried I won't be able to handle the responsibilities of the throne, of course she's afraid that I'll get hurt on such a perilous journey!' He put his hands on his hips and smiled widely. 'Then that'll just have to be another thing to prove to Mother, that she needn't protect me any more. Once she watches me brave the terrors of the forest and the dangers of the mountains, she'll be delighted to see me claim my destiny!'

He spun in an ecstatic circle, stepping on a trailing trouser leg and tripping into the arm of the couch. He realized he was shaking; this must have been the excitement Brutus felt when *he* was about to pledge his heart. Maybe Mother would hang an enormous portrait of Robbie in the Sceptre Room too, right next to his!

The confusion in Robbie's brain was ebbing away like water down a plughole. Mother loved him, and he was still able to pledge his heart – everything wrong had righted itself in the space of a minute. Yes, Mother was worried he might try and make the deathly dangerous trip through Bleak Forest, and he hated to worry her, but he had no choice.

Sometimes, thought Robbie, *evil people like me*

have to do scary things in order to succeed.

Then Robbie noticed that Devon had collapsed on to the couch and was rocking back and forth while spouting high-speed gibberish under her breath.

'Devon,' said Robbie, 'are you okay?'

Devon looked up through the crazed strands of hair stuck to her face. 'Young master,' she said. 'I really don't think this is a good idea. If the Queen finds out I was the one who told you where your heart is, she'll kill me for giving you the informa— for putting your life at risk. And my father, though he's probably not in your good books at the moment . . .' Devon trailed off and looked at her shoes.

Robbie nodded thoughtfully, then smiled again. 'Don't you worry, Devon,' he said. 'I promise that Mother will never find out that you were the one who told me. Cross my, um . . . metal thingy.'

'But, young master,' said Devon, 'I can't ask you to *lie* to the Queen! Think of the trouble you'll be in if she finds out!'

'What can she do?' said Robbie. 'I'm her son. Besides, keeping each other out of trouble – that's what friends are for.'

Devon parted her moist hair and gazed up at Robbie. 'You consider us friends?'

'Well, after this, definitely.'

Robbie watched as a tiny smile teased the corners of Devon's lips.

CHAPTER SEVEN

Robbie had wanted to leave at exactly midnight, but he overslept. So, at exactly three thirty-nine, while the sky was still a rich navy peppered with blackbird song, he slipped out of bed and quietly got dressed.

There was something about the castle at night that unnerved Robbie. It was as though there was something with him other than the castle rats, something following him through the dark as he crept down the familiar passages transformed by deep shadow. The portrait wing was lit sparsely with torches, the flickering firelight sending Robbie's shadow slicing across the faces of his long-dead relatives.

He felt the eyes of the portraits before he'd even stopped to look up. There they were, gazing down at him with gleeful sadism in their yellowy irises. Robbie saluted them. He hadn't met half the people on the wall, and couldn't even name the other half, but somewhere deep in his bones he knew that they would be proud of his mission. He nodded at the portraits and continued part one of his long quest: sneaking into the Sceptre Room.

And it was there, at the Sceptre Room doors, that Robbie encountered his first obstacle.

The Sceptre Room doors were heavy. *Very* heavy.

He hadn't anticipated just how heavy they'd be – Mother had always made them look so light, so easily movable. In fact, she could fling the doors open with barely a flick of her sinewy arms. Even the minuscule Devon could push them open by herself. Robbie tested one by leaning against it. It didn't budge an inch. He then used both arms, pushing as hard as he could, which resulted in a creak that set his teeth on edge.

Robbie looked up and down the dimly lit

hallways; it was of the utmost importance that he made as little noise as possible, but if he kept going at this rate he wouldn't leave the castle before sunrise. He pushed again and the door let out a long, agonizing *creeeeaaaak ...*

'Did you hear that?'

Robbie stopped pushing and stood very still. Somewhere far down the corridor he could hear footsteps on the flagstones – the guards on the night watch! He'd been heard!

He looked around frantically, trying to spy something, *anything* that could help him.

'Quiet! I think it came from over there ...'

The footsteps quickened, and Robbie saw torchlight in the distance, growing brighter and brighter. If he didn't do something now, he'd be caught and that would be it, finished before he'd even begun ...

There was a metal vase a few feet in front of him, an old family heirloom, on a pedestal next to a set of stairs leading down. Like a rabbit darting from a fox, Robbie shot forward, grabbed the vase and, with a silent apology to his ancestors, threw it down the stairs.

The vase made an echoey *clang, clang, clang* as it

bounced down each stone step of the stairway. Amid the resounding clatter Robbie raced back to the Sceptre Room, and with all the grace of a daddy-long-legs in flight, he threw himself at the doors.

Smack.

The doors only opened a few inches, but a few inches were enough for Robbie's skinny frame. He peeled himself off the door and slipped inside. The Sceptre Room was lined with portraits, and Robbie yanked one off the wall and thrust it into the gap between the door and the door frame, just before it could close.

He pressed his ear to the door, hands clasped over his mouth to silence his gulping breaths. The guards had reached him; he could hear footsteps just outside. His metal heart ticked faster and faster.

'Downstairs! I heard a crash!'

More footsteps.

'It was a vase. Must have fallen off the pedestal. Rats?'

'Probably, but if it is I don't want to wait around much longer. Have you seen the size of those things?'

The footsteps disappeared down the hallway and

Robbie breathed out, every part of him deflating as he fell back against the doors. He composed himself; this was only the first step of the mission after all, and it wasn't even complete.

The dim light of the Sceptre pulsed the room slowly from green to black, green to black. The humming was louder than Robbie remembered, or was it just that everything was quieter now in the dead of night? It didn't matter. What mattered was the mission.

Robbie's arms pricked with goosebumps as he walked towards the Sceptre. His scalp tingled as his hair became even more static than usual. He was less than a foot away from the pedestal when he stopped. It was one of those feelings that sits in your gut, the kind of feeling that could be anything from regret to apprehension to something you ate. Then a question flitted into Robbie's head before he could swat it away:

Am I doing the right thing?

As quickly as the question had appeared Robbie shook it out again. *Of course* he was doing the right thing. Bringing the Sceptre with him was the most efficient way he could think of to pledge his heart, and really, what was so bad about it? Or rather, what *wasn't* so bad about it? – stealing was what any evil person would do, and he was evil, right? Stealing's just part of the gig – why, it was absolutely *tiny* compared to the things he was going to do as head of the Sinistevil empire!

Robbie's eyes flicked momentarily to Brutus' portrait and he swallowed. Did Brutus ever wonder if he was doing the right thing?

Robbie ignored this thought and decided to think as little as possible for the remainder of the mission, otherwise it would take all night. He slipped his drawstring bag from his shoulder and approached the Sceptre. He reached out and paused, his hand hovering mere inches above the silver rod. Had he imagined the jewel's glow pulsing brighter just then? And that strange magnetic feeling in his hand, almost as if the metal in the staff was calling him to hold it . . .

Robbie shook his head, then took a deep breath and scooped up the Sceptre as quickly as possible. A static shock stung his hand, but he ignored it as best he could as he dropped the Sceptre into his bag.

He was about to pull the drawstrings to when he

noticed the tapestry directly above his head. There was something odd about it, but what? Then he realized: the bottom of the tapestry, just below the second verse, was frayed and uneven. From far away it looked deliberate, a style choice on behalf of whoever had stitched the verses in the first place, but up close Robbie could see that it had been torn. *What's there to tear?* thought Robbie. *There's only two verses.*

Robbie decided that this was a mystery best saved for a time when he wasn't trying to disappear into the night, and he turned back to his bag. As he pulled the drawstrings closed, the room fell black. His goosebumps disappeared, and his hair flattened slightly.

Feeling his way, Robbie placed the first of his handwritten notes on to the Sceptre's now-empty pedestal. He then shuffled back towards the double doors, trying not to make his boots squeak on the marble floor as he did. He slipped through the gap made by the portrait and, taking a deep breath, made his way towards the tapestry of Lazarule Sinistevil.

The chill of the late-night breeze brushed Robbie's face as he emerged at the other side of the tunnel. He stretched his legs and looked around. He'd never seen the truffle tree in the dark before. Somehow it looked a lot less inviting than it did in the bright sunlight with Layla. In fact, the silhouette of the heavy trunk against the moonlit night looked ominous and foreboding.

But Robbie didn't have time to be pondering trees. Creeping as silently as he could in his oversized boots, he took the second and final note and, brushing aside some low-hanging boughs, pushed it into a hole in the tree trunk. He was dimly aware of the shuffling noise his over-long trousers made as they dragged through the dirt, but he ignored this; there was no way Layla's family were going to hear anything from this far away.

As he took one last look at the truffle tree, he thought of Layla and sighed. She'd understand. In fact, she'd be the first to understand; she was his best friend, after all, and she did have a life apart from him. But that didn't mean he wasn't still going to miss her.

He shook his head – this level of sentimentality was not suitable for a young tyrant at all! These were the exact emotions he was going to have to squash down if he was ever to lead an evil army. *Hmm*, thought Robbie, *hopefully the Sceptre will help with that*.

With this final thought, he pulled a map out of his bag and turned in the direction of Bleak Forest.

CHAPTER EIGHT

Robbie had never been into town before in his life, let alone after dark. It was strangely quiet, much quieter than he'd expected it to be. He'd imagined taverns overflowing with people, loud singing and drunkards brawling in the streets. However, the street he was walking through was oppressively quiet, the kind of quiet made by a people who are desperately *trying* to be so.

In fact, that was entirely the case; due to the town's curfew, the people of Waning definitely did not want to be caught out of bed after hours. If anyone was skulking around the cobbled streets and thatched houses, they wanted to run into Robbie about as much as he wanted to run into them.

Robbie pulled down the hood of his cloak and let the breeze play with his hair. He had to admit, his mission was going surprisingly smoothly. All he had to do now was keep walking in the direction of the treetops, which he could see peering over the low houses before him. The Bleak Forest. His next stop...

Robbie leapt at the sound of heavy boots, and yanked his hood up before darting into an alleyway. He peeked out from the shadows, pulling his cloak tighter around him. Two guards marched down the road, coming closer and closer to the alleyway. Robbie felt beads of sweat emerge on his forehead as he silently watched the guards pass. Once the clanking of their armour and the pounding of their boots dissipated down the street, Robbie stepped anxiously from the alleyway. He looked up and down the street once more, before resuming his journey.

The houses grew sparse and the cobbles beneath his feet became compact mud, which in turn became dry yellow grass. Eventually, as he walked further and further from the town, the straw-like yellow turned to thick green and Robbie's footsteps squished as he crushed the dewy grass underfoot. The houses were far behind him now, and there – directly ahead – was a gate.

It wasn't a large gate, or a particularly impressive gate. It was merely a weather-worn contraption set in a rusted metal fence which stretched out as far as Robbie could see. One simple gate separating Sinistevil Castle and the wilderness of Bleak Forest.

And there, right in front of him, was the forest itself.

Robbie stopped by the fence and looked up. The trees grew close to the gate, barely a minute's walk away. The sun was already starting to rise and the dark grey of twilight made the trees look like stone; giant ashen monoliths with arms reaching and clasping each other. They were so intertwined that Robbie couldn't tell where one tree started and another finished. He swallowed. It was more than he'd imagined the forest would be, more . . .

Frightening? Imposing?

Robbie settled on *big*. The whole thing was an awful lot *bigger* than he'd anticipated.

But this was it. This was where his journey *really* began. He reached out and placed one hand on the gate, the cold from the metal melting through his palm. He shivered, then pushed.

'HEY!'

Robbie let go of the gate and spun around. Was it one of the guards? Had they followed him?

There, in the near distance, was a dust cloud barrelling down the path towards him. As it came closer it began to take shape, transforming from an angry blur to something a lot more human-ish, until finally Robbie could make out the patchwork form of Layla.

For a moment Robbie's thoughts were lost in complete panic; what should he do? Should he run? No, there was no point in that – Layla was already clearing ground with her immense speed, she'd catch him and pin him to the floor before he'd even made it through the gate. Robbie swallowed, and waited as she closed the distance between them.

As she got closer Robbie was afraid she wasn't going to stop – in fact she didn't stop marching until her nose was nearly touching Robbie's. Her chest heaved as she stared darkly into Robbie's eyes, her own umber ones betraying all the fury of a wildfire. Robbie didn't say anything. He didn't think he was capable of speech, and for the first time that night he found himself hoping Mother *would* catch up with him and save him from whatever fate this angry, silent Layla held in store for him.

Then Layla pulled a crumpled note from her pocket and thrust it at Robbie's chest.

'What is *this*?'

'Um,' said Robbie. 'I thought the note was self-explanatory.'

Layla's eyes shimmered with rage. She uncrumpled the note and read aloud. '*Dear Layla. I may not be around for a while as I am off to the Sunken Mountains to retrieve my heart and take the throne. Hopefully won't be too long, see you when I get back, Robbie.*'

She crushed the note in her fist and threw it on the ground. 'I couldn't sleep, and I saw our tree move. I come outside to find you *leaving in the middle of the night*? You were going to travel through the most dangerous forest in all of Waning to get to the most dangerous mountain range in all of Waning, all by yourself, with absolutely no warning, and *all I got was a stupid note?*'

'I didn't want you to worry!' whimpered Robbie.
'Well, I'm worried!'

Layla's nose was actually touching Robbie's now,
her shoulders rising and falling as her eyes bored into
his. Robbie didn't have time to argue; the sun was
already rising, the sky growing lighter by the minute.

'Layla, I . . .' he stuttered. 'This is something I
have to do. I am a Sinistevil, and as a Sinistevil I need
to go on this journey right now, before dawn, no
questions. I know it's . . . I'm sorry.'

Layla stared at him a moment longer. Then she
sighed and brushed the tight curls out of her face.

'You've never been travelling before, have you?'
she said.

'Yes, I have, actually,' said Robbie with a proud
smile. 'I've been to nearly every wing of the castle.'
Layla raised an eyebrow, and Robbie shuffled his
feet. 'It's a very *big* castle.'

'I'll take that as a no, then. You're going to need a
companion.'

Robbie watched as Layla narrowed her eyes and
bit her lip. *Oh no*, he thought, *this is Layla's thinking
face.* She only used that expression when trying to

decide something extremely important.

A look that would crack stone flashed across her face. She crossed her arms.

'I've decided. I'll come with you. I'll teach you how to set traps and light fires, all the things you should know. First of all, I need to pack.'

She turned and started walking back up the pathway towards the town.

'Layla, no!' called Robbie. 'I don't need any help! I'm evil enough to be able to – to *scare* fires into being, and – and of course I can hunt. I'm a Sinistevil! Besides . . . I couldn't ask you to do that. I know your parents will struggle with the harvest without your help, and I couldn't ever ask you to risk your life for me!'

Layla spun on her heels. 'Risk *my* life?' she snapped. 'You wouldn't last a *second* in Bleak Forest! You're not *asking* me to do anything, Robbie Sinistevil, this is a favour.'

Robbie ran up the pathway, tripping on his trouser legs as he caught up to her. 'I *can* do this, you know. I'm a Sinistevil, we do tough things like this all the time. It's in my blood, I can't help it. Besides, I'm a lot more resilient than I look.'

– 84 –

'Oh, good,' said Layla. 'Because you look about as resilient as a wet tissue.'

Robbie sighed. 'Is it because I tripped over my trouser legs just then?'

'It's because you're my friend. And if this is as important as you say it is, I'm coming to help you. End of.'

Robbie started to argue, before realizing that he actually didn't want to. He smiled. 'Thanks, Layla.'

'And after I've helped you survive the forest and you become King, maybe we can make some kind of a deal.' Layla grinned.

Robbie narrowed his eyes. 'What kind of deal?'

'Never you mind,' said Layla. 'Give me fifteen minutes, I'll be quick.'

And off she ran back to the town and out of sight. Robbie sat by the fence while he waited. Once again he felt relieved; as much as he didn't want to admit it, he couldn't help but wonder if he should have asked for Layla's help in the first place. After all, what were friends for, if not to accompany you on a daring journey filled with insurmountable odds and possible death?

Fifteen minutes later, Layla reappeared with a bag

on her back and a heavier pair of shoes. She stopped in front of Robbie and nudged his arm.

'You really have your heart set on this journey, huh?'

Robbie hesitated. 'Well . . . not quite, but yeah.'

'Then let's go.'

Robbie nodded. Taking a deep breath, he turned towards the gate to Bleak Forest. Together, the two placed their hands on the gate and pushed.

CHAPTER NINE

The morning was absolutely glorious, which instantly put the Queen in the foulest of moods.

The way the sunlight crept through a gap in the curtains made her physically sick; she didn't need to open them to know the sky was perfectly blue and cloudless, the *worst* kind of sky in her opinion. She pulled a pillow over her head and tried to go back to sleep.

But she couldn't. Something was bothering her. The weather? – no, it wasn't that, it was a noise – a very, very quiet noise coming from just outside her bedroom door. People were muttering, shuffling about, making the kind of increasingly irritating sounds people make when they are trying to be as quiet as possible.

The Queen pulled the pillow off her face and threw it to the floor. Something was going on in the castle. Not only that, but something was going on that the staff were trying to *hide* from her.

She clawed off the covers, stormed to the bedroom door and threw it open, revealing two terrified servants in the hallway. Both gasped at the sight of the Queen first thing in the morning, greasy hair on end, nightgown alarmingly askew.

The Queen growled, 'What is going on?'

The servants glanced at each other with frightened eyes, but said nothing.

'I have been awoken early on a particularly beautiful morning for this,' snarled the Queen. 'You will tell me what is going on right now or I will cut off your hair and use it to tie you to my balcony so I can personally watch you get cooked by the sun. *Talk. Now.*'

The servants trembled, then one said with a shaky voice, 'It's the young master Robbie, my mistress – he's not here.'

The Queen stared deep into the young girl's eyes, which were quickly filling with tears. 'Then where is he?'

One servant opened her mouth, before the other one interrupted, 'We're not sure, my mistress.'

The Queen watched as the two servants glanced from each other to her as rapidly as rabbits trying to figure out which way an oncoming carriage was going to go. This gave the Queen the distinct impression that she wasn't being told the whole truth. Which, of course, meant that she had been *lied to*. And if the Queen had been lied to, there were going to be definite consequences.

She slammed the door and got dressed. Moments later she re-emerged, her face set with a grimness reserved for particularly serious situations. Something was going on behind her back and she was going to find out what, no matter how many servants she had to tie to the balcony.

The hallways and corridors of Sinistevil Castle were much too quiet. She was being avoided – not just avoided, as the servants tended to do that anyway. No, they were actually hiding from her.

She turned left into the kitchens, which were completely empty. She stalked the tiled floors until she found a large cupboard next to the pantry. She opened the cupboard door, revealing five servants wedged in amongst the food like petrified sardines.

'Good morning, my mistress,' said a servant whose face was lodged beneath the armpit of another. 'Would you like some breakfast?'

The Queen slammed the cupboard door and left the kitchen, turning right towards the Sceptre Room. She rounded the corner and there was Devon standing next to the door, wringing her hands while sweat trickled steadily down her face. Devon looked up at the Queen and smiled broadly, her lips quivering like a twitchy centipede.

'My mistress!' she squeaked. 'How pleasant to see you this morning! I trust you've had breakfast?'

The Queen ignored her and reached for the Sceptre Room door. Like a flash of terrified lightning Devon intercepted, appearing between the Queen and the door with a frantic smile.

'Would you like some tea?' she cheeped.

'I will find out what's going on, Devon,' the

Queen hissed. 'So get out of my way.'

'What's going on?' said Devon. 'Oh – why, it's most perplexing – you see, the young master has gone missing and no one knows—'

'I meant what's *really* going on, you sentient grub!' snapped the Queen. Then she paused. A coldness started to travel up her gut and into her throat. 'Why are you outside the Sceptre Room?'

Devon blinked the sweat out of her eyes, then cleared her throat. 'Well, you see . . . the Sceptre . . . it is . . .'

A white-hot panic seized the Queen's brain. She picked up Devon and threw her several feet to the left, before flinging open the Sceptre Room doors and sprinting across the marble floor until she reached the Sceptre's pedestal.

It wasn't there.

But the pedestal wasn't completely empty – there was a slightly crumpled piece of paper. The Queen's mind was spinning in a thousand different directions. It took her hand numerous lunges before she finally grasped the note, unfolded it and held it with shaking hands up to her face.

Dear Mother,

I hope you're having a lovely morning!

I have decided to travel to Doctorcerer Clampit's surgery in the Sunken Mountains in order to retrieve my heart. Please don't worry, I'm an excellent navigator so I should be back in no time!

In the meantime, I hope the knowledge that I will soon be able to pledge my heart will bring you some comfort.

Also I took the Sceptre.

Lots of love,

Robbie xxx

Robbie had the Sceptre.

He was going to get his heart back.

Robbie had the Sceptre.

The note dropped from the Queen's hand and floated slowly to the floor. Devon crept over to her.

'*How could this happen?!*' screeched the Queen. 'Where did he get the idea to do this?!'

'I don't have a clue, my mistress,' said Devon, who was now sweating so badly she was making puddles on the marble. 'The guards have already been dispatched to the Bleak Forest gate, maybe they'll catch him before he gets too far . . .'

'No,' said the Queen as her spinning mind slowed to a gentle turning. 'No, it's going to be all right. Because I forgot, you see. I forgot that Robbie is an idiot.' The Queen grabbed Devon's shoulder and laughed. 'He's an idiot! He won't last a day in Bleak Forest, all on his own! In fact, he won't last *five seconds*!'

She laughed again, a high cackle that bounced off the walls of the Sceptre Room.

'I've done it, Devon!' she cried gleefully. 'And I didn't even have to lift a finger! Now all I need to do is retrieve the Sceptre from wherever he drops—'

Just then the doors opened and in marched the guards, their metal armour clanging on the hard floor. The head of the group approached the Queen and fell to her knee with a clank as she held out another crumpled note.

'We found it at the gate, my mistress,' said the guard. 'No sign of the young master.'

The Queen flattened the note and skimmed it, her smile twisting downwards.

'He has help,' she muttered. 'He's not alone, he's

got some commoner to help him?' She groaned as she crumpled the note in her hand. 'Of *course*, he managed to make a friend. How pathetic. Although now he may not die as quickly as I'd hoped. Hmmm . . .'

'We could go after them, my mistress,' said the guard. 'We could have them back by sundown.'

'No!' snapped the Queen. She didn't want to have to prise the Sceptre out of the hands of some cocky guardsmen who fancied their luck with the most powerful evil weapon in the universe. 'No,' she said. 'Leave. Now!'

The guards jogged from the room, *clank clank clank*, and closed the door.

Devon cleared her throat and said, 'What should I do now, my mis—'

The Queen held up her hand and Devon swallowed her words. Without the hum of the Sceptre, the room felt oddly empty, like a vacant coffin.

Wednesdays were usually Devon's favourite days, and by favourite she meant five per cent less anxiety-inducing than every single other day in the castle. Wednesdays were the days that Devon would sneak to the dungeons to say hello to her father.

Her father never said hello back, but that was entirely due to the gag, and he only didn't wave because of the heavy chains holding his arms to the dungeon wall. However, these facts never seemed to dampen his smile (at least Devon assumed he was smiling) and his eyes always lit up as Devon recounted her day in a babbling five-minute slot before she was called to her many, many other duties. She knew her father understood; he'd been head servant too once.

The day that Robbie disappeared from the castle just happened to be a Wednesday, and Devon could really have done with babbling to her father about it. Instead, she was in the Sceptre Room, standing tight-lipped and rigid as the Queen's brain silently generated wicked ideas to implement on her son.

'Devon.'

Devon risked a glance at the Queen. Her mistress's face was no longer upset. It was dark, her eyes half closed and the corners of her mouth set downwards like that of an angry trout. But she looked calm, collected. She had a plan.

Devon started to sweat again.

'Yes, my mistress?'

'Follow me.'

The Queen set off at her usual high-speed pace and Devon quickly trotted behind her. Her little legs buzzed with the effort of keeping up as the two flew through the main corridors, taking a left, a right, two more lefts. They eventually reached a small, dusty wooden door, nestled between two broom closets. The Queen pulled a key from her belt and forced it into the keyhole. The door unlocked with a sickening squeal, revealing a narrow stone staircase winding upwards. Devon gulped as she followed the Queen through the doorway.

It was strange; Devon had lived and worked in the castle her whole life, but she'd never, ever seen this wing before. It looked beyond old, the light grey stone of the walls and floor veiled in thick cobwebs. Every footstep kicked up dust as they climbed the increasingly narrow stairway, sunlight struggling in through ancient windows encrusted with a yellow frost of grime. Devon felt as though she was travelling through the insides of an extremely old mothball.

Finally, they reached a door, one so coated in cobwebs that entire families of thick-legged spiders ran for cover as the Queen's shadow fell over them. Devon wished she was one of those spiders, able to scuttle away from the Queen and disappear into some hidden crack in the wall.

The Queen thrust her hand through the webs and turned the door knob, which snapped off in her hand. She hissed through her teeth. 'These doors haven't been opened in decades,' she said, and she threw the door knob over her shoulder and kicked in the wooden door, sending it flying from the door frame and crashing into the room. Devon coughed and spluttered as another onslaught of dust attacked her nostrils.

Once the dust finally settled, she was able to see over the Queen's shoulder into the room itself. The small, narrow room was packed with shelves, all of which spilled with a myriad of dusty objects. However, Devon couldn't make out what anything was, due to the layers upon layers of dirt and neglect.

The Queen pushed through the room, almost knocking over entire shelves as she manoeuvred her body between the endless piles of everything. 'Shame everyone became so afraid to go to war with the Sinistevils,' she called over the clattering. 'I would *love* to dig out some of these toys again.'

She found what she was looking for; Devon could tell from the way she stopped so suddenly at the back of the room, her yellow eyes lighting up in a way that made Devon's insides tremble. The Queen reached out and plucked two objects from a shelf so laden it looked about to collapse. She turned around and Devon saw them: two grey orbs which fitted comfortably in each of the Queen's palms. The Queen blew away the dust, revealing their opaque bronze matte finish.

Devon leapt out of the way as the Queen barrelled towards her.

'Hands!' barked the Queen. Devon held out her quivering hands and the Queen thrust the orbs into them. The Queen then lifted the door, which now had a large crack down the middle, and wedged it back into the door frame.

'Now,' said the Queen. 'To the aviary.'

Devon waited until the Queen had forged ahead before she let her shoulders droop.

Back down the winding staircase and across the castle, up three flights of stairs and to the left lay the Queen's aviary. The room took up an entire wing and was filled with her pride and joy: her crows. They were called crows by a very loose definition, but of course not even the most seasoned ornithologist would have argued bird species with the Queen. The crows were big, the size of eagles, with beaks the size of their wings and talons even bigger than that. Their greasy black feathers were permanently ruffled, their eyes a gleaming fluorescent green.

Devon always thought they could have passed for Sinistevils themselves. The birds were terrifying, they were majestic, and Devon hated every single one of them. She was in charge of feeding the beasts, and they could never seem to differentiate between food and the feeder.

Of course, the Queen felt entirely differently about her beautiful babies.

'My gorgeous little darlings!' she called as she reached out to the birds, caressing their wings and scratching their scraggly heads. The crows hopped to the Queen and danced on their perches, nuzzling her hand with their beaks. One let out an ear-splitting *CAW* as the Queen tickled its chin. *Gosh*, thought Devon, *they even* sound *like the Queen*.

'Orbs!' squawked the Queen.

Devon thrust out the orbs. The Queen plucked one and placed it carefully on a large bird bath. 'One for me,' she said. She took the other, then cooed to one of her crows, which jumped happily on to her arm. The Queen held her out hand, and the crow held out its gigantic claw.

'And one for you. *Pouch!*'

Devon quickly rummaged through the shelves of the aviary until she found what the Queen had barked for: a small pouch made from a translucent mesh. She ran it to the Queen, who snatched it from her hand.

The Queen dropped the orb into the small pouch, which she then tied gently to the crow's claw. Once done she leant close to the crow's head and spoke, her voice low and terrible like faraway thunder. 'Go to Bleak Forest, find Robbie and bring me back the Sceptre.'

Devon could have sworn the crow nodded its head. The bird was readying itself to jump when the Queen held a stern finger to its beak. 'Do *not* kill him!' she said severely, before adding, 'But if you were to accidentally rip his hand off – well, what are we to do?'

The crow cawed loudly, then hopped from the Queen's arm and beat its ragged wings, flying out of the castle and high into the sky. The Queen ran to the other orb on the bird bath and Devon stood on her toes to see over her mistress's shoulders. The dirt on the orb moved and spun, turning the surface from bronze to . . .

No, Devon realized. The surface wasn't changing colour – it was beginning to show them something, patterns and movements. Devon leant closer and recognized some of the shapes: clouds rushing past, glimpses of the town from high above. The orb wasn't manufacturing these images, it was transmitting what the other orb could see from the see-through pouch of the crow.

'Find Robbie!' called the Queen. 'And bring back my Sceptre!'

The sky spun and suddenly the town below grew bigger and bigger. Devon felt her stomach lurch as the crow dived so it was level with the rooftops, frightened peasants scattering at the sight of it. One particular peasant caught Devon's eye, and she fought back a whimper.

It was a young man dressed in black, with a shock

of messy black hair sticking out all over the place. Surely Robbie had made it further than the town by now?

The crow seemed to recognize the Sinistevil too, as it swooped down like a winged nightmare. The boy turned around, and his cry of fear filled the room, exciting the other crows, which jumped and squawked, a flurry of noise and feathers. Devon bit down hard on her lip. But just as the crow was about to reach the boy the Queen leant in towards the orb and screamed:

'NOOO!'

Devon could see the boy's face now, a pale acne-marked face which was most certainly not the green of a Sinistevil. The bird pulled up and soared back into the sky, beating its wings in a forward thrust towards the forest.

The Queen picked up the orb and pushed it into Devon's hand with such force that she almost fell over backwards.

'You!' snapped the Queen. 'Watch this! Tell me the *second* it finds the boy! I may not be able to squash the little insect but I can at least stop him from pledging his heart and ruining my empire!'

Devon nodded. 'Yes, my mistress. Of course, my mistress.'

'And if you speak a word of this to anyone . . .' the Queen smiled a mean smile, 'well, maybe I'll forget to keep the rats away from a certain dungeon cell.'

Devon nodded her head quickly. She hadn't needed the Queen to give her a reason not to talk; it wasn't the first time she'd heard this threat. The dungeon rats were not something to be taken lightly, nor was the fact that they obeyed only the Queen.

With that, the Queen stormed from the room and slammed the door behind her, leaving Devon amid the floating feathers of the frantic aviary as the angry crows cawed. She sighed and looked down at the orb, watching the world fly by in the palm of her hand.

CHAPTER TEN

'Robbie Sinistevil, will you pick up your bleeding feet?'

There was another crash as Robbie fell sprawling into a gorse bush.

'I'm fine!' he said, spitting out thorns.

Something tugged at his arm and suddenly he was in the air, hovering a few inches off the ground. Layla let go of his arm and he landed on his feet.

'Wow, isn't this something,' he said, picking a few thorns out of his face. 'Who knew undergrowth could be so thick? Brutus probably did. Did you know that Brutus used to hunt in this very forest with Mother? He was an expert hunter. Did you know that?'

'Yes,' said Layla sourly. 'You've told me three times already.'

'Oh, sorry,' said Robbie, dragging his foot out of another patch of gorse. 'Did I tell you that he used to make his own path through the forest by removing the undergrowth with his bare hands? That's what Mother says anyway, and I believe her – did you see how big his muscles were? You can probably tell from the size of my cloak . . .'

'Can we talk about something else?' said Layla, kicking aside a tangle of roots.

'Like what?'

'*Anything.*' She turned to Robbie and pulled a twig out of his cloak. 'Not that I don't love hearing about the brother who levelled my village seven times before I was born, but we *have* been talking about him all morning.'

'Sorry,' said Robbie. 'I get carried away when I talk about Brutus. He never got carried away, though – did I ever tell you that his train of thought was always impeccably focused—'

'Maybe this undergrowth will get better when we

find the path,' said Layla loudly.

'This *is* the path.'

Robbie swung the bag from his shoulder and rummaged. After a few moments he pulled out the map and pressed his pointy nose against it. 'Yep,' he said. 'This is definitely it.'

Layla crossed her arms. 'How is it that a boy who's never left the castle in his entire life is able to read a map so well?'

Robbie pulled a black metal compass from his pocket and held it flat. 'I've been training to lead an evil army since I could walk,' he said. 'Map reading was always my favourite. Mother even said it was the thing I was least awful at. Not bad, eh?'

He looked up, that big goofy grin slathered across his soil-smeared face. He couldn't help it – he was optimistic. The sun was out, or at least it looked that way; the trees were so thick it was difficult to tell, but the greenish glow of the rays attempting to shine through the leaves was more than enough to light their way. His clothes may have been torn and his face may have been cut by brambles, but as far as he was concerned the journey was going exceedingly well.

'Come on,' said Layla, kicking at a thick root

which snaked across the forest floor. 'I don't want to stand still for too long. We don't know what's out here.'

It was strange, but Robbie had never seen Layla so nervous before. It was almost enough to make him start doubting himself – but he couldn't, not when the journey was off to such a good start. Holding the map out in front of him, Robbie marched ahead, before being quickly snared by another patch of brambles.

'I'm fine!'

Robbie scooped up the map as he struggled to his feet.

'I bet it's those shoes,' said Layla. 'They're at least seven sizes too big.'

'They fit fine,' said Robbie, beaming. 'They were my brother's.'

Layla nodded. 'So they're *definitely* too big.'

'Of course not,' said Robbie, brushing off the map and striding ahead of Layla. 'They fit perfectly. Once I've put on about ten pairs of socks, I can't even feel them slip!'

'Have you ever worn a pair of shoes that actually fit?' said Layla. 'I could always make you some.' She gasped and her eyes grew wide. 'Purple ones! Not bright purple, that would clash with your skin, but something deep and rich ...'

Robbie blinked. 'I don't know what you mean,' he said. 'My feet fit in these. They're Sinistevil shoes, and I'm a Sinistevil, so ...'

'They'll be regal, but practical,' said Layla. 'Graceful, yet durable, and you'll only need to knot the laces *once.*'

A patch of sky burst through a gap in the trees above them, and Robbie paused to bask in the beautiful daylight. What a fine day to start a journey on! Future historians would celebrate this day; maybe artists would even paint pictures of Robbie Sinistevil embarking upon this most evil of journeys with rays of sunshine pouring down his robes. Then a thought occurred to Robbie, and he frowned. Thinking back to the paintings in Sinistevil Castle, he couldn't actually remember a single one of them being set in glorious sunshine. In fact, most of them had storm clouds with great flashes of lightning zigzagging across the background. Maybe storm clouds would have been more appropriate for a journey as evil as Robbie's?

Robbie bit his lip. But he *liked* sunshine . . .

'Did you see that too?'

Robbie looked over to Layla, who was frowning at the sky. 'What?'

'I thought I saw something overhead.'

'Like a bird?'

'Looked a bit big.' Layla shook her head. 'You're right, it probably *was* just a bird. Who knows how big the animals grow out here in the forest?'

The two walked out of the patch of sunshine and back into the warm green shadow of the thick trees. Robbie sighed. 'Did you know that Brutus could chop down about thirty trees a minute with one hand—'

'I can't believe you actually stole the Sceptre,' said Layla quickly. 'Maybe you *are* evil after all.' She laughed, and Robbie didn't quite understand the joke, but laughed along anyway. 'What do you think your mother's going to do? I bet the whole castle will explode when she finds out!'

'I don't see why it would,' said Robbie. 'I left a note. How did *your* parents take it when you told them you were leaving?'

Layla looked away briefly, an awkward smile on

her lips. 'I, ugh, actually don't know. I pulled your trick and left a note myself. They'll understand, though. They know how important this is to me. I just hope they'll be able to bring in the harvest on their own, we don't *all* have superhuman brothers made of muscle.'

Robbie slipped the compass into the pocket of his cloak and folded the map under his arm. He felt a sudden pang of guilt squeeze his chest. It was all well and good *him* leaving – it was his idea, after all – but Layla's parents were probably much more afraid for their daughter. How would they feel about their only child travelling deep into the forest with a person as evil as himself?

He wanted to say something, but couldn't quite pick out the words. It was then that he noticed, in the distance, that the green had changed colour. Under his feet the undergrowth seemed to be thinning, the vines and roots weaving to the side like rivulets. Layla had noticed too, and together they sped up, kicking aside leaves and twigs as they ran towards the patch of bright light just up ahead.

It was a clearing. Robbie shielded his eyes from the searing sunlight and smiled. After such deep shade with only intermittent puddles of sun, he could have bathed in that sunlight all day long.

'Robbie.'

Robbie turned around. Layla was standing on the threshold between the trees and the clearing, her face obscured by dark green shadow. 'Come here,' she said. Robbie walked out of the light.

'What is it?' he said.

'Do you hear that?' said Layla, her voice hushed.

Robbie listened hard. 'What am I supposed to be hearing?' he said.

'Exactly,' whispered Layla. 'I can't hear a thing either. It's almost like there's nothing living here.'

Robbie shook his head quickly before the nerves could kick in. 'It's fine,' he said. 'Come on into the light, it's a lot less . . . creepy.'

Layla folded her arms. 'I'd have thought you'd like creepy, being so evil and everything.'

Robbie put his hands on his hips. 'I *do* happen to like creepy, thank you very much. It's just that I'm so used to things being creepy all day in the castle, it's nice to have a change of scenery.'

Layla looked unconvinced. 'I'm going to go and make something,' she said. 'Don't go anywhere.' She jogged off the path and began testing the low boughs of some of the trees.

Robbie turned back towards the clearing. He could hear the breeze high above, which was loud against the silence of the dense trees. He filled his lungs with the thick smell of leaves and dirt, throwing back his head to take a deeper breath. Then he saw it – the black dot flitting from one candyfloss cloud to another. *It* has *to be a bird*, thought Robbie as he squinted against the sunlight, but Layla was right. It did seem big. There it was again, circling so high Robbie couldn't even make out the species. *Maybe a hawk or something*, he thought, *readying to dive for its food*.

That was when he noticed another sound below the breeze, a sound which was gently pushing at the edges of his attention. Robbie concentrated, the weight of the Sceptre in his bag pulling at his shoulder – that was it, the Sceptre, humming softly as it lay against his back, almost like a voice trying to whisper something in his ear . . .

'Robbie!'

Robbie jumped as Layla appeared from behind a tree and skipped into the clearing, smiling with unabashed pride as she held out a very large flat stick.

'Cool, huh?' she said.

Robbie looked at the stick. 'Yes. That's a . . . cool stick, Layla.'

Layla narrowed her eyes. 'It's a *sword*,' she said, holding it up to Robbie's face. 'See where I've wound the vines here? That's the handle! And I sharpened the point a bit too.'

'Hm,' said Robbie. 'Do you reckon that thing will help us catch any food?'

Layla frowned tetchily. 'Yes, I think this *thing* will help us catch food! You could look a little more impressed, I made this in about a minute!' Layla looked back at her attempt at a sword, which already looked close to snapping, and frowned sadly. 'It's all right, isn't it?' she said doubtfully. 'What do you really think?'

Robbie smiled as widely as he could. 'I think it has character.'

Layla looked even sadder. 'Oh.'

'Why don't we stay here a minute?' said Robbie quickly, swinging the bag from his shoulder. He pulled open the drawstrings to look at the map, and the sun glinted off the emerald jewel of the Sceptre like a bright green spark.

Just then a shriek from above tore through the clearing. Robbie and Layla looked up as a shadow crossed their faces. Robbie was frozen by a rush of dread; something about that noise was awfully familiar.

He didn't have time to think, however, before the flurry of feathers was diving down upon them.

CHAPTER ELEVEN

Robbie hit the ground as the bird swooped, its talons ripping through his hair as he quickly ducked. He flipped on to his back and whipped his head left to right.

'Layla?' he cried.

'I'm here!' Layla shouted, and Robbie spotted her curled into a ball a few feet away. 'Does it think we're food or something?'

Robbie felt his shoulder and his eyes widened. 'Wait, my bag!' His eyes frantically scanned the clearing as the bird circled above. There it was – the bag, just to the left! 'Yes!' cried Robbie as he jumped up and dived towards it. As soon as he started running, the bird stopped circling.

'Robbie!' yelled Layla, scrabbling to her feet. 'Watch out!'

CAW!

Just as Robbie's hands grabbed the bag strap, so did a pair of enormous talons.

'No!' cried Robbie as the bird took flight – or at least it tried to, but Robbie was clinging furiously to the bag. However, the bird was strong, and Robbie was already on his tiptoes. If he could just pull back hard enough . . .

He stepped on the back of his robe, and the world flipped upside down as Robbie tripped, pulling the bag loose from the bird as he fell backwards and landed with a bump. The bag, along with the Sceptre, flew back over his head, skidding through the dirt and out of the clearing.

'Oh, no!' said Robbie as he crawled on to his knees. Where was it? He couldn't have lost the Sceptre already! What would Mother say?

The bird had flown higher now and was circling the clearing once again.

'What are you doing?' shouted Layla as she ran

towards Robbie. 'Get to cover before it dives again!'

'I can't find the bag!' said Robbie, spinning wildly in search of it.

'Forget that,' cried Layla. 'Duck!' Robbie took one look at Layla's face and dropped to the ground, just in time to see Layla pull back her arm.

'Hi-YAH!' Layla's sword flew from her grip like a boomerang. It wasn't a graceful throw, Robbie had to admit, watching as the stick spun erratically through the air like a lightning bolt. Its trajectory curved as the bird finally spotted what it was looking for and took a serendipitous lunge, right into the boomerang-sword's path.

CAW-*AGH!*

THUD.

After a few moments, Robbie opened his eyes. He didn't know what had fallen from the sky. He only knew that it had hurt when it hit his head.

'Robbie, are you okay?'

Layla was shaking his shoulders. Robbie looked up at her and smiled.

'I'm absolutely fine,' he said. 'Completely peachy. Possibly concussed, but otherwise splendid.'

'Are you going to get up?'

'That depends – is anything else about to fall from the sky to put me in a coma?' He sat up. 'Not that I'm whining or anything, it's just that I'd rather be prepared. Wait – my bag! The Sceptre!'

Layla helped Robbie to his feet, and he immediately began scouring the clearing. Then he saw it, just in the shadow of the trees, resting snuggly against a trunk. He almost cried with relief.

'Thank goodness!'

He ran to the bag and peered through the drawstring opening. There was the Sceptre, still glowing serenely as though it hadn't almost been lost for ever only moments ago.

Robbie sighed deeply, then pulled the bag on to his shoulder and walked back to Layla. There on the ground lay what looked to be some sort of massive raven, or maybe a vulture; either way, it was the biggest, scruffiest black bird he had ever seen. Thanks to Layla's stick, it now lay motionless in the dirt.

'Wow,' gasped Robbie. 'You're a really good hunter, Layla!'

'I don't know if this counts as hunting,' said Layla, frowning. 'We don't really do stuff like this back home, normally we just set a trap. I'm surprised this worked, to be honest.'

Robbie almost said *Me too*, but thought better of it. 'I think I've seen birds like this before,' he said, scratching his chin. 'But I don't see how it could be . . .'

'Whatever it is,' grinned Layla, '*I* think it looks like dinner. Robbie? What's wrong?'

Robbie stared at the bird, at its lifeless eyes and twisted wings, and a horribly familiar ache prodded at his stomach. It was an ache he remembered from being in the kitchen after Mother had returned from one of her many hunting trips, having laid her slain carcasses on the table for the chef to clean. It was an ache Robbie had always assumed was indigestion.

Layla read his face. 'Don't tell me you're not okay with hunting. How else did you expect us to eat?'

Robbie ignored his stomach and turned to Layla. 'I'm absolutely fine with hunting,' he said. 'I'm a Sinistevil, remember, and there is nothing we like more than death and destruction, especially that of small . . . helpless creatures . . . like birds and stuff. I'm sure that if Mother had ever taken me out hunting I would have thoroughly enjoyed it.'

Layla nodded to the bird. 'You don't look like you love dead animals.'

Robbie bit his lip. 'Well, I do, so there. I love dead animals. The deader, the better. If I didn't, who would I be?'

'Robbie,' said Layla simply. She knelt down and pushed the bird off her sword, making its lifeless head flop to the side and hit the floor with a thud and a wet squelch. Robbie retched. Layla gave him a sideways glance.

'That was a retch of happiness,' said Robbie. 'It was a happy retch.'

'I'm sure it was,' said Layla. She regarded the bird for a moment. 'It looks like your mother.'

'Hey!' said Robbie. 'You can't just say things like that about people's . . . Oh, yeah, it does a bit.'

Something else occurred to Robbie in that moment; the sense of familiarity he'd felt upon hearing the bird call from above the clearing. He stared at the bird intently.

'*Robbie? Robbie? Is that you?*'

Robbie stopped staring at the bird and blinked at Layla. She blinked back at him.

'The bird is talking to me, Layla.'

'Yeah, I think it is.'

'*Robbie! Down here!*'

Robbie knew that voice. He frowned at the bird. 'Devon?'

'Robbie!'

Layla was pointing at something shining in the centre of the clearing, not far from where the bird had landed. Robbie ran over to it and squatted down to see what appeared to be an orb reflecting something: a face. He leant over the orb, putting his nose close to the surface, and as he did so the voice became louder.

'*Robbie!*' said the voice. '*It is you! I'm so glad you're safe!*'

A smile spread across Robbie's face, and he lifted the orb so Layla could see it too.

'Devon!' he said. 'How nice of you to drop by!'

'*Oh, young master,*' gasped Devon, wiping away a torrent of sweat with her sleeve. Her freckles seemed even darker, or was it that her face was paler? '*I'm so relieved you're okay!*' she said. '*But, where's the crow? How did you manage to keep it from tearing your hand off? Did it take the Sceptre? Also, who is the girl with the bloody stick?*'

'Oh,' said Robbie. 'This is Layla. Layla, Devon, Devon, Layla. Devon's a friend.'

'Ah,' said Layla, waving the stick. 'Hi.'

'So, Devon,' said Robbie. 'When did you become a tiny floating head?'

'*There isn't time for this, young master!*' squeaked Devon. '*The Queen will be back any minute! She's already looking for you, the orb you're holding is so she can see where you are . . .*'

'Aww,' said Robbie. 'Mother's keeping an eye on me! See Layla, I *told* you she wouldn't be angry about the Sceptre.'

'I don't think that's the point of this, Robbie,' said Layla. 'I think Devon's trying to tell us that your mother is spying on us. And I don't think we were meant to see that bird coming.'

'What do you mean?' said Robbie. 'Mother was just dropping us off a snack. She must be worried about my hunting skills – that's another thing I'll just have to prove to her. Can you put Mother on the orb, Devon? I want to say hi!'

'*Actually, young master, I'd rather not call the Queen right now . . .*'

'If she's busy, that's fine.'

'*Robbie!*' Devon clasped her hands over her mouth, her eyes wide. Then she whispered, '*I'm so very, very sorry for snapping at you, my young master, but the truth is that you and your friend are in terrible danger. The Queen wants the Sceptre back, and I think she has some very nasty plans up her sleeve to make that happen. The crow was just the start – I'm afraid I can't do anything to stop her, but I may be able to help you from here!*'

'Wait a minute,' said Layla, pushing Robbie's head out of the way so she could scrutinize Devon. 'How do we know the Queen's not with you right now?'

Devon sighed. '*I'm afraid I can only give you my word. I'll try my best to keep her oblivious.*'

Robbie leant closer to the orb. 'You mean you want to help me get my heart back?'

Devon winced, her face shining. '*It seems incredibly dangerous, terrifying and not particularly bright to dispute the Queen's orders, but . . . I suppose I'd prefer you for a master over her.*' She immediately straightened her spine and began to babble. '*No offence intended, of course – I live to serve* all *my masters.*'

Robbie and Layla looked at each other. Layla raised her eyebrows, while Robbie knitted his and gave a nervous half-smile. Layla nodded and turned back to Devon.

'I guess we can trust you for now,' she said.

Devon nodded, her chin trembling. '*Thank you. I have to go now, the Queen will be here any moment . . . Please be careful!*'

'Bye, Devon!' called Robbie, but the face had already disappeared. 'Well,' he said. 'That was unexpected.'

Layla nodded to the orb. 'I think you should put that in your pocket.'

'You're right,' said Robbie, slipping the orb into his robe. 'For safe keeping.'

'I was thinking more so your mother can't see where we are.'

Robbie hitched up his bag and frowned. 'Why on earth would we do that? How can she help us if she doesn't know where we are?'

Layla opened her mouth to speak, then stopped. 'Never mind. Tell you what.' She walked over to the crow and lifted its limp body by the neck. She grinned. 'Why don't we forget our monumental troubles while I teach you how to cook a bird?'

CHAPTER TWELVE

There was a terrible knot in Devon's stomach, and she knew exactly why it was there; it was the unbearable guilt at having to hand over the orb to the Queen. But what choice did she have? She knew the consequences of disobeying the Queen's orders. Devon was just trying to stay alive, a feat which was proving increasingly difficult as she broke the news to the Queen that not only had her precious crow completely failed to take the Sceptre from Robbie, but it had also become lunch. The Queen had not taken this news well.

'That slimy little nitwit!' The Queen slammed

her fist against a bird bath. Devon's hands shook as she held out the orb so the Queen could watch the blackness of Robbie's pocket with increasing agitation.

'He thinks he's fooled me, doesn't he?' she muttered through gritted teeth. 'And now he's *mocking me* . . . No. No, he's not smart enough for that.' The Queen's hunched shoulders slumped as she slowly calmed herself. 'Perhaps my beauty was too gentle in her pursuit. Perhaps it's time for more *violent* measures. Devon, come!'

Devon hopped to keep up with the Queen as she marched from the aviary and down a winding flight of stairs. They didn't stop at the first floor, or the ground floor, as Devon had hoped they would. Instead, they travelled further and further down, and as the increasingly narrowing staircase grew darker and greyer Devon felt an unease fill her gut; they were travelling towards the dungeons.

A small set of stone steps led them to a passageway blocked by two guards. The guards didn't have time to step aside before the Queen had grabbed each by their helmets and thrown them back over her shoulders. Devon winced as the clanging of metal armour on stone echoed endlessly down the halls behind her.

The passageway was dark, lit only by dim torches which were placed sparsely along the cobweb-infested walls. Relief and fear fought for a place in Devon's head; her father's cell was all the way over on the other side of the dungeons, nowhere near where they were, but she wasn't too happy about where they'd ended up instead. She made a habit of avoiding this dungeon passage in particular – it was where the giant rats lived. Even the regular rats of Sinistevil Castle (which were already extremely large) stayed away from *this* passage.

Devon felt something thin and wiry brush her ankle. She forced herself not to think about it.

The Queen slowed down, and Devon noticed that her clanking footsteps now sounded more like *crunching* footsteps. She looked down, saw the tiny piles of bones, and immediately looked up, adding the bones to the list of things she was not going to think about.

A few more awful crunching steps later, the

Queen stopped. Then she stooped low and dragged her fingernails across the wall, small sparks jumping from her fingernails as a few loose bricks rattled beneath them. She found the one she was looking for, a crumbling discoloured brick with several scratch marks of its own, and prised it from the wall. Devon shuddered at the rustling from the hole, but it quickly died away when the Queen began to speak.

'You've seen what's been happening in *my* castle,' hissed the Queen into the hole. 'The castle I let you live in, that I let you *feed* in. Now you do something for me. Find Robbie and bring back the Sceptre. You may hurt him as much as you want, maim him for all I care, but *do not kill him* – and don't damage the Sceptre!'

A chorus of squeaks reached a crescendo, then disappeared down the wall like a gust of wind through a tunnel. The Queen stood up straight, her spine making a quick succession of clicks as she righted herself. She turned to Devon with a look of complete and utter distaste.

'Watch the orb,' she said, her voice low with warning. 'They may be the fastest creatures I know, but I don't trust them one bit not to bite straight through the Sceptre.'

She picked a piece of wall from her fingernail and flicked it. The gravel bounced off Devon's head and clattered down the passageway.

'Apologies for speaking, my mistress,' Devon whispered, trying not to hear the rats scuttling in the wall beside her head. 'But is this to say that you'll keep Robbie safe? At least, from being killed?'

The Queen glowered down at Devon, who began to regret every word she'd ever said in her life. But instead of throwing her down the passageway as Devon suspected she would, the Queen sighed.

'*Their wicked life shall not be spared*,' she quoted, filing the nail of her little finger against the wall. 'Terrible things happen to Sinistevils who deliberately kill their heirs. You may wish to look up my Great-Aunt Rheumatia in the Sinistevil library, I believe her head is still mounted in the east wing. However, there are more *annoying* clauses –' the Queen looked over Devon's shoulder and scowled, '– but we shouldn't have to deal with any of those. As long as the rat does its job.'

The Queen stalked past Devon, and Devon ran

to catch up with her – she very much disliked the idea of being left alone in this part of the dungeon. She had never seen one of the giant rats in person, and she wanted to keep it that way.

CHAPTER THIRTEEN

Plucking the bird hadn't been too bad. Robbie had just about managed to disassociate the bird corpse from a living bird, and the continuous action of pulling the feathers was actually quite therapeutic. Maybe he was getting the hang of this whole hunting lark after all.

Then came the innards.

After Robbie regained consciousness, Layla sent him away. She wasn't happy about having to do all the work, but agreed that the food would be ready much quicker if she didn't also have to provide constant first aid.

So Robbie ventured out of the clearing, back into the green shadows of the forest to collect some firewood. He waited until he was certain Layla couldn't see him, before planting his head on a tree trunk, closing his eyes, and sighing deeply. He kicked at his shoes. No matter how hard he tried, he just couldn't stop thinking about Layla's parents, who were probably worried sick. He imagined them sitting at home, reading Layla's note and wondering if they'd ever see their daughter again.

He knew that as an evil prince he shouldn't be worrying about the lives of peasants, but that wasn't the only problem. The other problem was that he was feeling worried at all. Sinistevils didn't *feel worried*.

Once again, the Sceptre hummed at his back. There was the whispering again, just quiet enough that he couldn't quite . . .

'Are you really *that* upset that I sent you away?'

Robbie jumped. Layla stopped smiling when she saw the look on his face.

'What's up?' she said. 'You don't look so good. I mean, I know you've just fainted like three times, but still.'

Robbie looked at his feet.

'I think you should go back.'

Layla crossed her arms. 'Really?' she said. 'Why?'

Robbie bit his lip as he fumbled for the words he wanted to say. 'I feel like . . . Well, as an effective evil leader, I need to know when to delegate and when to go it alone, and . . . I am making an executive decision to send you home to your parents.'

Layla stepped forward. For a moment she simply stared at Robbie, as though she was trying to work out a complicated sum. Then she punched him hard in the shoulder.

'Ow!' cried Robbie. Layla squared up to him, nose to nose.

'As I said before, Robbie Sinistevil – I made my *own* decision and came here of my *own* volition, *as a favour*. You can't send me away, because I'm not one of your subjects and I'm not following your orders! I *want* you to find your heart, and while I think it's incredibly sweet that you're worried about me and my parents, I would kindly ask you to butt out and let me do my thing!'

Her voice echoed off the otherwise silent forest walls as Robbie opened his mouth, closed it, then opened it again.

'I'm not *worried* about you,' he said quickly as his eyes flitted back and forth. 'I don't do things like *worry*, because – because I'm evil, obviously.'

Layla shook her head. 'Yeah, well, you do *a lot* of things evil people don't normally do.'

Robbie frowned. 'Like what?'

Layla put her hands on her hips. 'Well, you're friends with me, for one thing.'

'All evil people need allies,' said Robbie. 'It's just common sense.' Robbie felt his stomach twist a little as he said this; he'd seen paintings of a few of Mother's allies, and he was hesitant to put Layla in the same category as any of *them*.

'How about the bird, then?' said Layla. 'You couldn't even kill it when it was *attacking* you!'

'I could hunt if I had the opportunity,' said Robbie, fiddling with his sleeves. 'I just didn't want to get Brutus' cloak dirty, is all.'

'You could always take it off,' said Layla, narrowing her eyes, 'if you're so worried about it getting dirty – not that you've been trailing it all through the muddy forest path because it's seven sizes too big, or anything.'

Robbie pulled his cloak tighter around him,

feeling his cheeks turn an even darker shade of green. Then he began to look around. 'In that case,' he said, rolling up his sleeves, 'I'll prove my evilness to you. I'll hunt my own food.' He bit his lip in concentration as he searched the nearby branches, trying extremely hard not to look at Layla.

Finally, there, just behind the trees – a thicket of bushes which boasted an excess of bright purple berries.

'Ah-ha!' called Robbie, charging towards them. He tried to pull off a branch, but the bush was more stubborn than it looked. Robbie pulled one-handed, then, with a quick glance at Layla, put another hand on the branch, then, an embarrassed moment later, a foot against the roots.

SNAP.

'See?' said Robbie from where he lay on his back, triumphantly clutching the liberated berry branch. 'Successfully hunted berries.'

'Well done,' said Layla, holding out a hand to help him up. 'How evil of you to wrestle those berries to the ground.'

'Thank you,' said Robbie, brushing the dry leaves from his trousers. 'Now for dinner.'

Layla frowned at the berries. 'Actually, Robbie, they look pretty poisonous.'

'And what of it?' said Robbie, picking the berries from the branch individually until he had a bright purple handful.

'Put them down, Robbie,' said Layla. 'You'll get sick!'

'Pah,' said Robbie. 'I am a Sinistevil. We are much too evil to be affected by such lowly poisons.'

Layla's eyes widened. 'Robbie, don't—'

But she was too late, Robbie had already thrown the berries down his throat without so much as chewing a single one. 'See?' he said. 'Perfectly *finnnnnneeeeuuuuurgh* ...'

There was a new knot in Robbie's stomach now, and he was fairly certain it was not an emotional one. *Yes*, he thought, *this one seems entirely more physical.* He wiped his brow and looked up at Layla, who looked extremely concerned.

'You've no need to look at me like that,' groaned Robbie as he clutched his stomach. 'This is just the evils in my stomach working out the poison from the— *huuuurrrgh.*'

Robbie doubled over and the bare branch

dropped from his hand. He saw Layla wave her hands in panic before sprinting over and skidding to a halt behind him. After a moment's frantic deliberation while babbling '*whatdoIdowhatdoIdowhatdoIdo*', she wrapped her arms around Robbie's abdomen and heaved once, twice, thrice . . .

'*HYAGH.*'

The berries flew out of Robbie's mouth like bullets, splatting a bright purple polka-dot pattern on the tree across from him. Both Robbie and Layla collapsed to the ground, back to back, gasping for breath. Robbie swallowed, then gagged. Everything tasted like berries.

'You know, I didn't mean to insult you before,' said Robbie, his throat still raspy from the berry-ejection. 'When I told you to go home.'

'I know,' said Layla. 'I'm sorry I got annoyed. I guess I was just a little upset at the idea of you not wanting me around.' She sighed. 'Which I know I'll have to get used to when you're King.'

'Of course I want you around!' said Robbie incredulously. 'I'm really glad you're here – especially now, with the berries and all.' Robbie frowned, suddenly uneasy for reasons he couldn't quite put his finger on. 'I guess they just didn't react well to the evil juices in my stomach.'

Layla sighed heavily, then got to her feet. 'Help me gather firewood.'

Robbie stood up unsteadily and scanned the ground for dry sticks.

'Actually,' said Layla, inspecting a couple of twigs, 'I've got my own reasons for being out here. It's not all about you, you know.'

'Oh?' said Robbie. 'Wait – the deal you mentioned, by the gate.'

Layla nodded. 'Yeah. I happen to be pretty tired of all this evil dictator nonsense, and I'm going to do something about it. I think I'd much rather someone like you on the throne, someone who's kind enough to look out for peasants like us. I have a list of ways I think we can improve Waning, and I'd feel a lot more comfortable approaching a King who'd actually listen.'

Robbie looked up. 'Well, of course I'd listen,' he said. 'It's what friends do.'

Layla smirked. 'Caring for your friends,' she muttered. 'How positively evil.' She looked back at Robbie and her smile turned bashful. 'Maybe I could even work my way up to Vice Evil Dictator and look out for Waning that way, make a few changes myself. That's the plan, anyway. I can even make my own uniform – the red ones I've seen through the castle windows are a bit gaudy if you ask me.'

Robbie's lips twitched into a smile. 'Vice Evil Dictator Layla Granite. Has a nice ring to it! I can't believe you thought I wouldn't want you around when I'm King – you're going to be my second-in-command.'

Layla shook her head, and Robbie didn't miss the way she tried to hide her widening smile. 'We'll set up camp here, I think. You start a fire, I'll bring the bird over.'

Robbie watched Layla disappear behind the trees before he let the smile slip from his face. When he was certain she couldn't see him any more, he dropped to his hands and knees and sifted through the dry soil until he'd managed to pick out a few large, sharp stones, about the size of his fist. He stood up, one stone held in his left hand as he stared hard at a tree.

Robbie had been one year old when Brutus died, so he didn't have any real memories of his beloved brother – just the stories Mother told him while comparing her two sons. One of Robbie's favourite stories was of a game they played together, where baby Robbie, propped against a wall (because he was useless, Mother always added), would watch as Brutus hurled stones at the squirrels who dared to jump the trees near the castle walls. The furry little creatures' ducking and diving was always futile; Brutus was a perfect shot.

Robbie looked up into the trees and tried to spot some animals. He narrowed his eyes as he inspected the branches, trying to spy another bird, a little squirrel, a woodlouse, *anything*. It was no use: the trees were completely empty. No matter, Robbie had an excellent imagination. He went about imagining a fluffy squirrel zigzagging through the branches. He took a deep breath and pulled back his arm, readying a throw that would knock the imaginary squirrel out of the tree with his expert aim ...

The stone made a soft thump as it fell from his hand, hitting the floor next to his feet. Something had stopped him from throwing it.

He tried again, this time with a slightly bigger rock, and he imagined that this particular squirrel had insulted his family name by throwing half-chewed nuts at the Sinistevil coat of arms. Robbie racked up all the anger he could muster, using this rage as fuel to smite the tiny insubordinate and . . .

Once again, he dropped the stone.

Robbie sighed and put his hand to his chest, feeling the now familiar *tick-tick* of his clockwork heart. He didn't understand it – he was evil, he *knew* he was evil – so why was he having so much trouble taking down an imaginary squirrel? Why on earth was it so difficult to just throw a stone at an animal that wasn't even there?

What was wrong with him?

Robbie heard footsteps behind him, and quickly started arranging the campfire as Layla brought over dinner.

CHAPTER FOURTEEN

'*R*obbie? Robbie...'

Robbie could taste dirt.

He opened his eyes, an action he immediately regretted. He rolled on to his back and tried to blink out the blobs of soil lodged in his eye sockets, but the way his eyes watered simply turned the soil to mud. *At least mud is good for the skin*, he thought as he spat out a mouthful of it and dislodged a twig from his front teeth.

Every joint, every limb, even parts of his body he didn't know he had *ached*. Robbie groaned; because he'd woken up in a fantastic mood every single day of his life so far, he'd always assumed he was a morning person. He was starting to suspect this had more to do with the fact that he'd always woken up in a king-size four-poster bed with satin sheets and goose-feather pillows, and *not* on a forest floor.

'*Robbie!*'

Robbie rubbed the mud from his eyes and looked around. The campfire on the edge of the clearing was still smoking gently, the bones of their dinner in a neat pile beside it. A little way from that was Layla, curled into a tight ball on top of Robbie's cloak, with the silky sleeve tied around her head as a makeshift hair wrap.

'What?' called Robbie, who was startled by his own croaky voice; it felt like a single night in the forest had aged him eighty years at least.

Layla stirred, then rolled on to her back and peered at Robbie through sleep-blurred eyes. 'What?'

'You called my name,' said Robbie.

'No, I didn't. *You* just woke *me* up.'

'*ROBBIE!*'

Both Robbie's and Layla's eyes widened – the orb! Layla sat up and untied Robbie's cloak sleeve from her head as she pulled the little brass orb from the cloak pocket. Robbie rushed over, and they both leant in until they could see the tiny freckled face of Devon, the tip of her nose pressed against the orb's surface.

'Good morning, Devon!' said Robbie, chirpiness seeping through his groggy veins as he took the orb. 'How are you?'

'*No time for pleasantries, I'm afraid.*' Devon's voice was a squeaky whisper. '*The Queen will be here any second!*' She peered over her shoulder nervously before pressing her nose back to the orb. '*She has allies – and she's sending them to you as we speak!*'

'Oh, wonderful!' said Robbie, pulling on his cloak. 'That's brilliant news!'

'No, it's not,' snapped Layla, who snatched the orb from Robbie's hand. 'Who are they, Devon? How long have we got?'

'*I'm so sorry,*' whispered Devon. '*She wanted them to reach you by morning. I wish I could tell you more, but if I'm caught she'll make a tapestry of my skin. Please be vigilant, young master and Layla, they could be anywhere!*'

With that, Devon's face disappeared. Layla thrust

the orb back into Robbie's hand and got to her feet.

'Come on,' she said. 'If the Queen's allies are on their way, I want to be as far from here as possible. Which way?'

Robbie put the orb back into his pocket and pulled the map from his bag. 'That way, down that path.' He'd barely finished speaking before Layla was on her way. Robbie scrabbled to his feet. 'Wait, wait,' he called. 'What about breakfast?'

'There's no time for breakfast,' said Layla without looking back. 'We've got to get moving!'

'Layla!' Robbie flung his bag over his shoulder, the weight of the Sceptre hitting him hard between the shoulder blades. He ran in front of Layla and skidded to a stop, blocking her way with his arms outstretched. 'Mother's sending allies – isn't that a good thing? We should wait here, maybe they'll escort us to the mountains!'

Layla huffed and began tapping her foot. 'I'm completely certain that if the Queen is sending people to find us, they're probably going to do us in.'

She marched past Robbie, who skipped to keep up with her.

'I don't understand why you think she'd do that!'

he said to the side of her head. 'She's my mother! The woman who's let me live in her castle for the past twelve years!'

'How kind,' scoffed Layla.

Robbie stopped and waited for Layla to notice he wasn't behind her. Once she'd turned around Robbie crossed his arms and narrowed his eyes.

'Why do you hate my mother?' he said.

Layla walked back down the path towards him. 'Well, other than the whole "her armies tearing down our houses for fun" thing, it's because she's an evil, tyrannical dictator and if anyone considers themselves a friend or ally of that evil woman, I don't want to meet them.'

Robbie frowned. '*I'm* evil and you still talk to me.'

'Not again,' said Layla, shaking her head. 'Robbie, we don't have time to keep doing this – you're not evil.'

Robbie clutched his bag strap tighter. 'Why do you keep saying that?'

'Why do you have to *be* evil?'

'Because I'm a Sinistevil! I . . .'

'Robbie!'

Layla's finger shot to her lips. Her eyes were wide,

and Robbie realized that she'd heard something, something close . . .

Layla gasped, then sprang forward and pushed him to the ground. The back of his head hit the floor with a bump.

'Ow,' he groaned, 'Layla, that . . .' But Layla was frantically pointing behind him.

'Rat!' she hissed. 'There was a rat!'

Robbie frowned as he rose shakily to his feet. 'I appreciate you looking out for my safety, but don't you think that might have been a bit of an over-reaction to a little—'

Layla grabbed Robbie's shoulders and spun him round just in time to see a long grey tail, the size of a large snake, whip behind a tree. Robbie turned back to Layla and gulped. 'Right,' he said. 'That did look a little larger than— AGH!'

Something whacked Robbie from behind and sent him flying through the air. He hit the ground hard and rolled through the dirt. He grabbed his arm where he'd been hit, where *something* had hit him; three long claw marks had ripped through his cloak. Robbie bit his lip and looked up as a long, high-pitched snarl weaved through the clearing.

'Oh,' breathed Robbie as he gazed at the most enormous rat he had ever seen in his life. 'That's quite big.'

Robbie had seen rats before. He'd often chased them for fun as they scampered in and out of the castle walls, up until they'd started to chase him back. However, as big as the rats of Sinistevil Castle were, he had never seen one quite *this* big. To make matters worse, the creature towering over him with grey matted fur and bright pink eyes did not look at all friendly.

Its beady eyes flicked from Robbie to Layla, front teeth protruding, its claws twitching with anticipation. Robbie squeaked as the rat's gaze locked on to him. With a horrifying squeal, it pounced.

Robbie rolled to the side, barely missing the rat's strike as he clambered to his feet. The rat didn't give him time to think, and took out Robbie's legs with its tail, sending him sprawling to the ground before it darted away.

Robbie leapt up, but when he felt for his bag his heart skipped a tick – it wasn't there! It must have fallen off when he fell. Suddenly a silver glint flashed in the corner of his eye, and he turned to see the rat pulling apart the drawstrings of his bag. The rat had the bag. *The rat had the Sceptre!* Without thinking Robbie dived at the rat and snatched the bag, narrowly missing the furious swipes of its claws as he sprinted away.

Robbie could hear it squealing behind him as he ran. He looked over his shoulder, and his oversized left shoe caught his right, and he flew forwards, right into . . .

SMACK!

Robbie lay on his back in a daze, his head pounding from where it had collided with the tree. The rat skidded to a halt and turned towards the helpless Robbie on the ground. Robbie clutched the Sceptre bag to his chest as the beast readied itself, thick saliva dripping from its razor teeth as it growled and bent, ready to pounce.

In his arms, the Sceptre hummed. Robbie heard it, felt the vibrations of it as he hugged the bag close. There was the whisper again . . .

No, thought Robbie as he struggled to his feet. If Mother saw him lying snivelling on the ground like this, she'd *never* think he was worthy enough to pledge his heart. She'd never even let him back into the castle!

Robbie stood up tall and faced the rat, which watched with interest as he tried to glare it down. However, Robbie's best attempt at a glare included rapid blinking and a quite significant chin wobble. The rat noticed this and snarled a gleeful snarl as it flexed its claws.

And then something happened. The Sceptre hummed and Robbie, for reasons he couldn't quite grasp, instinctively reached into the bag. The green glow of the jewel lit Robbie's face as he undid the drawstring, and the forest seemed to grow suddenly quiet. Words chattered through Robbie's head at full speed as his hand drew close to the Sceptre, words which didn't quite feel like his own. *Fight the rat, hit it with the Sceptre, bludgeon it, HURT it. That's what Brutus would do, that's what would make Mother proud, do it, do it now!*

Robbie's hand closed around the silver staff.

'AAAAARGH!'

A boot struck Robbie's shoulder and his head snapped up, unsure of what he'd just been doing, what he'd just been *thinking*. He was only aware that Layla was flying through the air, her stick-sword raised high above the rat as she cried out an earth-shaking battle cry—

SNAP.

Robbie gasped as Layla's sword snapped over the rat's head like the twig it was. Layla tumbled on to her backside, holding up her sad half of a stick with a look of horror. The rat had been irritated before. Now it was *angry.* It turned to Layla and readied itself to pounce.

'No! Layla!'

Robbie leapt forward, snatching up the pointy half of Layla's broken sword and throwing it at the rat. It bounced pitifully off its head, but it did the trick – the rat turned to Robbie and snarled, leaping forward just as he stepped out of the way. The rat saw the tree behind him much too late . . .

Robbie's hands flew to his eyes. He couldn't see, but he did hear the squeak, and the thump.

'You can look now.'

Robbie slowly lowered his hands. Layla was standing over the rat, which was curled into a tight, unmoving ball. She turned to Robbie sadly.

'It broke my sword.'

'I'm really sorry,' said Robbie.

'You looked like you were going to fight it,' said Layla. 'What made you stop? You could have hit it with the bag!'

'I'm sorry, I don't know what happened,' said Robbie, his cheeks flushed. 'Something just . . . didn't feel right.' He shook his head, drew the bag closed and brushed himself down. 'What a random attack. I wonder what Mother's allies will make of it when they get here?'

CHAPTER FIFTEEN

Sinistevil Castle was, for a moment, completely silent.

Then it erupted.

Devon's ears were starting to hurt from all the screamed death threats and obscenities that flowed from the Queen's mouth as she stormed about the aviary. Feathers fluttered down as the crows jumped and cawed in response to the Queen's tirade.

'*THAT SHOULD HAVE WORKED!*' the Queen wailed as she flung a bird feeder into a wall. '*THAT THING SHOULD HAVE TORN THE SCEPTRE FROM HIS FILTHY LITTLE HANDS!*'

Devon didn't know what else to do, other than stay perfectly still; if she didn't move, the Queen might not fling *her* into a wall along with the bird feeders.

The Queen picked up a perch and sent it flying through the aviary window. There was a crash and a distant scream from the ground floor. The sounds of innocents screaming seemed to calm the Queen down, at least; the rise and fall of her back and the clenching and unclenching of her claw-like hands steadily began to slow. Eventually, she turned to Devon, who instinctively began to shake.

'They got lucky,' growled the Queen. 'But their luck *will* run out.'

She knitted her fingers and narrowed her eyes. Then she smiled, a slow, wide smile which revealed her black teeth one by one. 'Well, then, I'm just going to have to employ some new tactics.'

Devon did not like the sound of the words *new tactics*. They made her shudder as she followed the Queen out of the aviary. Moments later they had travelled through the castle back to the trinket room in which the Queen had found the orbs. This time, however, the Queen moved slowly as she clambered through the dusty shelves, careful not to knock anything over as she conducted her meticulous search. The urgency with which she had crashed through the room yesterday was gone, and in its place was a dark calculatedness which frightened Devon oh-so-much more.

Devon crept into the room behind the Queen, anxious to make as little noise as possible as she side-stepped the dusty artefacts which jutted from ancient shelves. But the floor was so cluttered Devon couldn't help tripping and falling into a bookshelf which was leaning so far forwards with weight it was a wonder it was upright at all. As though responding to Devon's silent pleas the bookshelf only wobbled slightly, and as Devon sighed heavily with relief her eyes fell upon a piece of neatly rolled fabric on the lowest shelf. She stared at it and frowned. Even through the layers upon layers of dust, Devon could see a familiar pattern to the fabric, something she had seen before very recently. But what was it?

She looked up. The Queen was still too engrossed in her own search to notice her. As quietly as she could, Devon took the fabric and gently unfurled it. A few spiders fell loose and scuttled away as the fabric unrolled, and once the small haze of dust around it cleared Devon's mouth fell open.

That's where she'd seen it before! No wonder it was hidden! Did Robbie know about this? If he didn't, he *should*. Devon quickly folded the fabric, ready to stuff it into the pocket of her uniform – and paused. She couldn't take it. What if the Queen found out she had it? Worse, what if the Queen caught her sending it to Robbie? If that happened, she'd never see her father again . . .

'Ah-*ha*.'

Devon jumped and shoved the fabric into her pocket. Fortunately, the Queen hadn't spotted *her;* she'd spotted something else.

At the very back of the room lay something tall and thin covered by a grey blanket. The Queen removed the blanket with a flourish that lifted a cloud of cobwebs and dust, revealing a podium rising to her shoulders. The podium seemed to be made from vines, thick sandy-coloured vines which wound around each other and culminated in a large marble skull. The Queen's eyes sparkled with anticipation.

'Oh, Devon,' she called, her voice dark and low.

'Come and see. You're going to find this quite fun.'

Devon gulped. 'Am I, mistress?' she said as she waded through the clutter.

The Queen smiled wider as she raised her hands over the skull. The skull itself was deep maroon, almost black, and as the Queen moved her hands over its smooth cranium the room became bitingly cold. Devon could have sworn she saw something glint in the skull's eye socket. She hazarded to speak, the sudden cold making her teeth chatter.

'W-w-what is it, m-m-mistress?'

'Hm,' smiled the Queen, her gaze transfixed on the skull's wide grin. 'A landline to some dear old friends. Another little trinket your father managed to source for me.' She shot Devon a look. 'In fact, *most* things in this room would be familiar to your father. A very useful head servant indeed – wouldn't have met half my most wonderful friends if not for him. I'm sure you're proud.'

The Queen said this last bit with a slimy twitch of her lips before turning back to the skull. Devon looked down at her brightly polished shoes. She felt awfully like her father's daughter, standing there doing nothing as the Queen contacted yet another creature that could hurt Robbie and Layla. She knew her father wasn't *bad*, his muffled and incomprehensible words always had a regretful quality to them behind the gag, and goodness knew she understood the complexities of having to follow the Queen's orders . . . but even so.

Her shoulders drooped.

The Queen stroked the cranium and whispered into where its ear would be if it had skin. Devon shuddered as the room grew suddenly even colder, and she had to blink to make sure the vines of the podium weren't *really* slithering upwards, further around the skull . . .

Then, as suddenly as it had come, the coldness melted from the room. The Queen clapped her hands in delight.

'They said they're free!' she trilled. 'How wonderful. Come, back to the aviary.'

The Queen turned and strode from the room, clicking for Devon to follow.

Devon was still quaking with nerves once they'd arrived back in the aviary. Fortunately, the Queen didn't notice; she was too busy coaxing a crow on to her arm. This particular crow was skinnier than the rest, hopping head first into multiple bird feeders before finally finding its way to the Queen. The Queen cooed as she stroked its head and whispered something into its ear. Devon didn't like the way her eyes glinted like barbed wire as she did.

The crow nodded and let out a loud *CAW*.

'Wonderful,' said the Queen sweetly, stroking the crow's head.

'We're sending another crow to Robbie, my mistress?' said Devon, an idea formulating in her head.

'Of course, you little imbecile,' snapped the Queen. 'It's the best way to send a message, after all.'

She won't be the only one sending something, thought Devon as her hand twitched next to her pocket where the fabric lay.

'Shall I attach another pouch, my mistress?' Devon already had a pouch in her hand before the Queen could even open her mouth.

'That won't be necessary,' said the Queen, ignoring Devon and making little kissy faces at the skinny crow's beak. 'I know,' she said to the crow. 'I know, my lovely, I'm sorry. But it's a very special job, very important, there's simply no way around it.'

Devon took a deep breath; this was her only chance. She made sure the Queen was still engrossed in fussing her babies, then surreptitiously kicked at a bird bath. The bath wobbled, and several crows cawed and danced in protest. When the Queen looked back at the commotion Devon darted forward and stuffed the rolled-up fabric into the crow's pouch.

'Sssh!' she hissed at the crow.

The crow cawed in response, causing the Queen to turn back to it and nuzzle its beak. *Please don't notice the pouch*, Devon pleaded inwardly, please *don't notice . . .*

'Poor little baby,' said the Queen as she lifted the crow on her arm. 'Not the brightest, but unfortunately perfect for this task.' The 'poor little baby' then took flight, swooping into a wall before righting itself and flapping self-consciously out of the window and into the greying sky.

Devon waited until the crow was out of sight before secretly sighing with relief.

'You don't spend decades leading an evil army without making a few interesting friends,' said the Queen, still staring into the cloudy sky. 'And wouldn't you know it – some of my *favourite* friends live in a particular forest.' She smirked. 'Let that idiot and his disgusting peasant friend celebrate their little victory. But as soon as the crow hits the ground, the fun will begin.'

CHAPTER SIXTEEN

Robbie didn't like standing around.

The sun had been swallowed by a sea of grey, their once-bright clearing now filled with shadow. Robbie looked down and gulped; the motionless body of the monster rat wasn't doing anything to calm his nerves.

Layla, however, was still trying to put her stick-sword back together, pathetically pushing the fractured halves against each other with zero success. Robbie clutched at his bag strap. 'Sorry to bother you, Layla, but do you think you could move just a teensy bit faster? Brutus always said that it was never wise to stay in one place too long, especially after an attack.'

Layla sighed sadly and dropped the two sticks. Robbie pulled his torn cloak tighter around himself as a breeze sifted through the trees and about the clearing. He turned towards the path, but stopped once he noticed Layla wasn't following him and was instead staring at the rat with intense fascination. He groaned inwardly, his anxiety turning to impatience.

'Layla, what are you doing?'

'Hm,' said Layla. 'I was just thinking . . . Do you reckon it's edible?'

Robbie retched, then turned to the path, which lay beneath a tunnel of trees.

'I really don't think we should be standing still,' he said. 'There might be more.'

'You're right,' said Layla, finally leaving the rat. 'This *is* a pretty poor effort from your mother. Just one thing that couldn't even kill us? I reckon she's got more waiting.'

Robbie frowned as Layla wandered past him, and his nervousness and impatience suddenly faded away.

'I still don't understand why you think that thing was sent by Mother,' said Robbie. Layla turned around and sighed exasperatedly, which made Robbie's hackles rise. He lifted his nose snootily. 'I'm part of an evil monarchy. There are all sorts of people out to get me, and I have no reason to believe that any of those people are my own loving mother.' By the look on Layla's face, Robbie realized he had probably spoken more snootily than he'd intended to.

Layla lifted her hands and shrugged. 'Well, let's go through the clues, then, shall we? The rat appeared out of nowhere, instantly went for *you* and tried to steal the Sceptre. Obviously, your mother doesn't want you to get your heart back.'

Layla turned to walk away again, and Robbie felt his cheeks grow hot. The Sceptre hummed softly and he felt the familiar thud of the staff against his back as he overtook Layla, spinning to face her before she could disappear into the tunnel of trees.

'Mother loves me, and loving mothers don't try to kill their only sons.' He hitched his bag strap further up his shoulder. 'So now that I've taken apart your ridiculous argument, we can forget about it.'

Layla's mouth fell open. Robbie thought she was going to say something, but instead she clamped her jaw shut and scowled as hard as she could. Robbie huffed as he turned around and strode ahead of her. This time it was Layla's turn to overtake him.

'I honestly don't understand you sometimes,' she said. 'You can be the nicest person in the world but the moment I call out your mother for—'

'For what?' said Robbie. 'Caring for me all my life? Giving me food and clothes?'

'She *didn't* give you clothes, though, did she?' snapped Layla, pulling on the corner of Robbie's sleeve. He yanked his hand away and Layla shook her head. 'You know what, the more I think about it the more I realize that it's an absolute miracle you turned out as kind as you are.' She narrowed her eyes. 'Or *were*, at least.'

Robbie scoffed. '*Kind?* Do I *look* kind? A Sinistevil is *not* kind! This is not the green skin of kindness!'

'If it weren't for that green skin,' said Layla. 'I'd have doubts you were a Sinistevil at all!'

Robbie thought he heard the Sceptre buzz louder – until he realized the buzz was actually coming from his pocket, along with a tinny sound like an insect trapped in a glass jar; the orb. Layla opened her mouth to speak and Robbie lifted a finger to stop her, an action which made Layla's jaw drop even further and her face fill with rage.

'Robbie, you little . . .'

'Devon!' said Robbie, holding up the orb to block Layla's face. 'Have you been calling me for long? I'm awfully sorry to have kept you waiting, I was just teaching Layla the correct definition of kindness and how it in no way applies to myself . . .'

'*We haven't got time to talk about whatever this is!*' Robbie jerked back from the force of Devon's shrill whisper. '*I can hear her on the stairs!*'

'Sorry Devon, I think there's something wrong with the orb,' said Robbie. 'The picture won't stop shaking.'

'I *can't stop shaking!*' cried Devon. '*It's going to come when the bird hits the ground! You'll need to get into the trees – but there's something else! I've sent you a . . .*'

Robbie held the orb closer to his pointy green nose. 'What bird? I don't get it.'

'*Listen! It's in the bird's pouch and I really do think it is of the utmost importance that you . . .*' Devon went silent, looked over her shoulder, then snapped back to the screen. '*She's coming!*'

The orb went back to its usual opaque.

'What was that about?' said Layla, crossing her arms. 'Another care package from your loving mother?'

'No,' said Robbie. 'She was talking about a bird.'

Layla looked into the sky and grinned. 'Speaking of which ...'

She bent down and picked up a stone as a loud *CAW* filled the air. Robbie looked up too and saw yet another large black bird circling the clearing. It was the exact same kind as the one from before, the one that'd attacked him and tried to steal his bag. He suddenly felt uneasy.

'Wait a minute, Layla ...'

'Don't you shush me again, Robbie Sinistevil!' said Layla, pulling back her arm. 'I'm catching us some dinner because *you* aren't evil enough to hunt!'

She released the stone, which hurtled through the air and missed the bird by miles. The bird, confused and distracted by the random flying stone, flew into a tree. It hit the floor of the clearing with a heavy *thump*.

Robbie followed Layla to where the bird lay. 'That still counts as me hitting it,' she grumbled.

'Absolutely,' said Robbie. 'See, this is why I don't hunt. It is entirely more evil to let nature take its course.'

Even as he said this Robbie couldn't help but feel a sting of sorrow for the poor bird lying on the ground in front of him, a bird that had done nothing wrong but fly irresponsibly. Layla noticed his teary eyes and smirked, making him look down quickly to hide his blush.

'I wonder what Devon was talking about when she said *it'll come when the bird hits the ground*,' said Robbie. 'I suppose she meant dinner?' He looked down, and frowned; what was that next to his foot? It looked like a piece of bunched-up fabric, but what was it doing in the middle of the forest? It was then that he realized it must have fallen off the bird – which meant it had come from the castle. Why had Devon sent them this? And why was that pattern so … familiar?

'See, *that's* why you can't hunt,' said Layla as Robbie picked up the fabric. 'Because you are too sensitive towards other living creatures, and that doesn't make you evil. It makes you *nice*.'

Robbie gasped, and angrily stuffed the fabric into

his pocket. 'How *dare* you!'

'You are! You are *nice* and *kind* and *sweet* and *lovely . . .*'

'Stop it! I'm not! I'm . . .'

A sound like whispers flitted through the clearing. Robbie and Layla stopped bickering and looked around. Layla reached down to pick up the bird – and it vanished.

The two stared at the spot where the bird had just been. Robbie straightened up and put his hands on his hips. 'Well, that was unusual.'

'Robbie,' said Layla, 'did the bird just get swallowed up by a hole in the ground?'

'Mmhmm,' said Robbie. 'I think that's exactly what happened.'

'Where's the rat gone?'

Robbie looked around. The rat's body was nowhere to be seen. 'Ah,' he said.

'Right,' said Layla. 'What did Devon say about getting into the trees?'

'It was something like— WAH!'

Robbie hit the floor hard, then scrabbled quickly to his feet.

'What happened?' said Layla, helping him up.

'Something touched my leg!' cried Robbie. 'No, it – it *pulled* me!' He pointed at the ground where he'd just fallen, but there was nothing there but a small patch of upturned earth.

Layla grabbed Robbie's arm and dragged him towards the edge of the clearing. 'Come on, let's get off the ground quick!'

Robbie watched as she caught a low-hanging bough and effortlessly pulled herself up. Robbie gripped his bag strap and shuffled his feet, the back of his shirt growing sticky with sweat.

'I, um,' he muttered anxiously, 'I'm not actually that good at climbing. And before you say anything, it's *not* because I'm not evil enough!'

'I didn't think it was,' said Layla from her branch. 'I thought it was because your mother never bothered to teach you how to climb.'

Robbie was about to retort when he heard a rustle from the centre of the clearing and turned his head – just as a mound of earth began to slowly upturn itself.

Robbie's legs started to tremble as he tested some of the lower branches. 'Maybe *your* mother was able to teach you how to climb despite being a busy farming peasant and all that,' said Robbie. 'But *my* mother had to concentrate on such things as ordering her evil armies about, so she couldn't possibly . . .'

'Did *Brutus* know how to climb?'

'Of course, Mother taught him as part of his basic combat training . . .' Robbie pressed his foot against the tree trunk, then paused. 'That doesn't prove anything! Now, if you could just give me a leg up . . .'

Something burst from the ground and Robbie spun round. There, searching through the soil, was a long sandy-coloured tentacle. It was thick as the branches Layla was hiding in, making no noise as it crawled endlessly out from beneath the ground. It snaked across the dirt and crept slowly towards the spot where Robbie stood whimpering.

He turned to run, but with a burst of soil appeared yet another tentacle, blocking his path. Robbie looked up at Layla with watery eyes.

'I'm fine!' he cried.

The tentacles stopped their slow meander and shot suddenly through the earth. Robbie jumped – too late, as one of the tentacles snagged his ankle and sent him sprawling face-first into the soil. He spat the dirt from his mouth and crawled away, just as another tentacle wrapped itself around his bag and pulled it from his shoulder.

'The Sceptre!' gasped Robbie, grabbing the bag strap tightly as the tentacle tried to wrestle it from his hands.

'Forget the Sceptre!' called Layla. 'Get over here!'

'I *can't* forget the Sceptre!' said Robbie through gritted teeth as the tentacle prised his fingers from the bag strap one by one.

SNAP! The strap broke and the bag flew from Robbie's grasp. The tentacles weren't moving slowly any more; now they were speeding out of the ground, and in seconds one had wrapped itself around Robbie's leg. Robbie struggled to no avail – his oversized boots were way too heavy for him to control any of his kicks. He glanced at the tentacle stealing his bag, and through a gap in the bag's opening he could see the green jewel of the Sceptre winking in the light. He reached out towards it.

'Leave it, Robbie!' shouted Layla, leaning as far down the branch as she could.

'I can't!' said Robbie as the vines wrapped tighter and tighter around his leg. 'I need it!'

'No, you don't!'

'Yes, I do!' Robbie swatted at a tentacle, which swatted back. 'If I lose it now, Mother will never think I'm capable of taking the throne!'

Robbie struggled fiercely for the bag, but with every passing moment it was dragged further from his reach. The ground beneath Robbie began to crumble away.

'Your mother doesn't care about you, Robbie!' cried Layla. 'Now grab my hand or . . .'

'Stop saying she doesn't *care*!!'

The Sceptre's jewel flashed green and hummed loudly as it was dragged slowly towards the now-gaping hole in the earth.

Robbie desperately tried to think. The Sceptre was getting further and further away; he could still hear it, but the hum was getting quieter and quieter, and all he knew was that if he lost it, he lost everything.

'Hi-YAH!'

Layla leapt from the tree and landed on the tentacles ensnaring Robbie's legs. With a squeal the tentacles unwrapped and scattered, slithering frantically across the ground. Robbie got up and ran to his bag, snatching the Sceptre out of it just as the rest of his belongings were swallowed up by the earth. The Sceptre's jewel flashed again as Robbie's hand met the staff, a buzz of energy shooting up his arm and disappearing just as quickly.

Layla was already up the tree again, arms held out, when Robbie noticed something. The tentacles hadn't immediately grabbed his legs again; in fact, the impact of Layla's boot seemed to have shocked them into some confusion. They were searching around the clearing, coming close but not directly, almost as if . . .

Ahhhhh, thought Robbie, *so* that's *why we needed to get into the trees.*

Against every instinct he had, he stayed perfectly still. He looked up at Layla and put his finger to his lips. Layla looked like she was about to kill him for shushing her for a *third* time, but Robbie quickly pointed to his eyes and mouthed: *They can't see.*

Understanding dawned on Layla and she nodded. Carefully and silently, she climbed down from the tree and stepped over the tentacles, which were still sifting sluggishly through the dirt. Very slowly, Robbie and Layla crept around the clearing and on to the path, into another tunnel of trees. Robbie held his breath until they were completely swallowed by the dark green shade, and then they both ran until the forest obscured the clearing altogether.

Finally they stopped, both doubled over and panting for breath. The only light around was the sparse spots of grey which managed to pierce the leaves above, and even that was dimming fast. When Robbie looked up, he could barely see Layla in front of him.

'That,' he gasped, 'was close.'

Layla wiped the sweat from her brow and looked at Robbie through narrowed eyes. 'It would have been much less close if your mother had taught you how to climb – or if you'd left the Sceptre.'

The Sceptre's light pulsed and Robbie scowled. 'Turns out I didn't *need* to climb, did I?'

'Whatever,' said Layla. 'Where's the map?'

Robbie reached for his bag, then stopped. 'Oh ...'

Layla's eyes widened. 'You grabbed the Sceptre out of the bag but not the *map*?'

'There's only one path, and we're on it!' said Robbie, putting his hands on his hips. 'So we didn't *need* the map, did we? You know, I thought you'd be a little more grateful to me for figuring out how to get away from those things.'

'You're right,' said Layla, crossing her arms. 'You managed to save both our lives without climbing *or* fighting. Running away when you're afraid? Not exactly an *evil* method, is it?'

'That doesn't prove anything,' said Robbie, biting his lip. 'And for your information I wasn't afraid. Sinistevils aren't afraid of anything.'

'Well, that's dumb.' Layla held her head high as she overtook him. 'What's wrong with being scared of scary things?'

Robbie tried to come up with an answer, but he couldn't.

CHAPTER SEVENTEEN

The tunnel grew even darker, the impenetrable leaves above them plunging everything into deep shadow. Robbie didn't mind this too much; the glow of the Sceptre was not quite bright enough to see Layla by, which made her much easier to ignore. Layla seemed to be of the same opinion as she plodded sulkily behind him. Neither had spoken to the other in a while.

Robbie held the Sceptre to his chest and felt the springs of his heart twitch and flutter. The glow of the jewel pulsed once. This frequent humming and pulsing hadn't escaped Robbie's notice, and only made him more frustrated as he wondered why. He sighed. It was at times like this he wished he had his brother to talk to.

It wasn't fair. Only Brutus could possibly understand the pressure Robbie was under. If he were alive, Robbie could have asked him all the specifics of the Sceptre and pledging his heart; he could have even asked Brutus how *he* managed to prove he was evil enough to take the throne.

Except Brutus had never *had* to prove himself worthy. Robbie's shoulders drooped. Brutus was born a Sinistevil for the ages; no one had ever doubted that *he* was the most evil being alive. He'd never had to prove he was capable of running an evil empire.

So why did Robbie have to?

Robbie tripped on his trailing trouser leg and bit his lip, hissing as he rubbed the now swollen spot with his tongue. He thought he heard an intake of breath, like Layla was about to speak. But she didn't. Robbie didn't like not talking to Layla. Somehow, it felt worse than arguing. He wondered then whether or not Brutus had ever fallen out with a friend.

He frowned. Had Brutus ever *had* friends?

A sound drifted above the soft crunch of shoes on the undergrowth. Goosebumps rose on the back of Robbie's neck as he realized the Sceptre was getting ever so slightly louder. Its low hum was now a constant, following him through the tunnel of trees.

I can hear you, thought Robbie, *but you have to tell me what you* want.

As sudden as whiplash, his thoughts swam back to his argument with Layla. She'd said Mother didn't care about him; she'd said it like it was nothing. Words started filling Robbie's head, words that weren't quite his own, as though someone else was whispering them in his ear. How could Layla understand? He was Mother's only son; of *course* she cared about him – she *had* to, which is exactly why *he* had to prove himself. He had to succeed, *Layla was just a lowly peasant girl and if she didn't understand then maybe he should just leave her alone in the deep dark forest where she'd be food for the—*

Robbie heard a whooshing sound, and the words disappeared. He saw an orange glow through the corner of his eye, and thought at first that the Sceptre was doing something different – but then he heard the crackle of fire. Layla must have made a torch.

Layla . . . had he just been thinking about her? He couldn't quite recall.

A pang of guilt shot through Robbie's chest as he thought about his friend. He knew one thing for certain: he would never have survived this long in the forest if it weren't for her looking out for him.

Robbie stopped walking and turned around. Layla stopped too, the torch in her hand casting a bouncing light on the trees around them. Robbie searched for the right words, but could only find three. His entire body deflated as his eyes welled with tears.

'She's my *mother*.'

Layla sighed and ran to Robbie. As soon as she was close enough Robbie wrapped her in a hug that lifted her off her feet.

'Ug, Robbie, okay, enough now.'

Robbie let go. 'I'm sorry,' he said.

'No,' said Layla. '*I'm* sorry. I was out of line. I guess it's just easy to forget that she's your mum.'

'I didn't have to be such an idiot about it, though,' said Robbie, and Layla gave him a sad smile.

'Well, it's not like we aren't under a lot of stress at the moment, is it?'

Robbie nodded, then collapsed against a tree trunk, sliding down until he was sitting in the dirt. 'Layla,' he muttered, before throwing back his head and wailing, 'why do all these horrible things keep coming after *me*?'

Layla sat down across from him and put her chin in her hands. 'They do keep coming after you, don't they? Almost as if someone—' Her head shot up. 'I'm not saying who, but almost as if *whoever they are* is sending things to take the Sceptre.'

Robbie groaned again, a long groan that echoed all the way down the pathway. That was when he noticed Layla staring at him. Or not quite at *him*.

'Whoa,' breathed Layla. 'Is *that* it?'

Robbie looked down at the Sceptre in his lap, realizing for the first time that Layla had never actually seen it before. 'Yeah,' he said. 'This is it.'

'Wow,' said Layla. 'I didn't think it would actually ...*glow*.'

'I think it's getting brighter,' said Robbie. 'It wasn't glowing this much when I took it.'

Layla frowned. 'Is that a bad thing? I mean, it's dark magic after all.'

'I should *hope* it's a bad thing,' said Robbie,

running his fingers across the vine patterns in the staff. 'Wouldn't be much of an evil object if it didn't do bad things.'

Robbie gripped the Sceptre and lifted it slightly. It was heavy in his grip. He gazed into its strange green jewel, and listened to its hum, and realized that although he'd been carrying it on his back all through the forest he'd never actually *felt* it like this before. Even though he'd picked it up in the Sceptre Room, he'd never truly experienced the full weight of it in his hands. The faintest buzz travelled through the metal and into his palms. He could feel it, the sheer *power* of it.

'I think,' he said in a small voice, 'it's been trying to talk to me.'

Layla said nothing. Then she awkwardly held up her hand. 'The torch is giving me splinters,' she said. 'I don't suppose you've got anything I can wrap the handle in?'

'I lost my bag when we got attacked by those freaky vine things,' said Robbie, before remembering something. He reached into his pocket and pulled out a piece of fabric, the one he'd found on the floor when he was talking to Devon. He carefully placed the Sceptre on the ground and the fabric on his lap.

'What's that?' said Layla, wiping her nose on her sleeve. 'Brutus' evil hankie?'

'It was on the ground before,' Robbie muttered as he unfurled the fabric. 'I think Devon sent it. You can use it, but I want to see what it is first.' The fabric didn't stop unfolding, and eventually it had covered his whole lap. There was something oddly familiar about the fabric itself, something Robbie couldn't quite put his finger on. The pattern on the front was random: strange etchings below a torn, frayed edge.

'What do you think it is?' said Robbie.

'I don't know,' said Layla. 'But I think you've got it upside down.'

'Upside down?' said Robbie, leaning so close to the fabric that it touched his nose.

'I'm just thinking of the patterns I sew on to clothes,' shrugged Layla. 'That looks more like the *back* of the pattern, where the needle goes in.'

Robbie nodded. He turned over the fabric, and his chest froze.

A four-line verse, just like the ones on the tapestry in the Sceptre Room. *That* was what was so familiar about it.

'What's wrong?' said Layla, her brow creasing as Robbie's eyes widened.

'In the Sceptre Room at home, there's this tapestry,' breathed Robbie. 'The last time I saw it I thought the design looked weird, like the bottom of it had been torn off – I think it *was*! This must be the part that was missing, the final set of instructions for when I pledge my heart.'

'You mean there's another verse to that weird rhyme thing?' said Layla.

'I don't know, I always thought there were only two! I pledge my heart and get filled with hate,' Robbie gasped. 'Maybe this is the final step to taking the throne!'

'Go on,' said Layla, her eyes wide. 'What does it say?'

By the mix of orange and green light, Robbie held up the torn piece of tapestry and read aloud:

'With heart and Sceptre side by side
An heir must act to seal their fate –
Destroy the one who comes before,
Complete the pact of blood and hate.'

The Sceptre pulsed and hummed loudly, like a swarm of bees coming close then immediately disappearing back into the darkness. The jewel flashed bright, then dimmed, once again giving way to the light of Layla's torch. Robbie and Layla sat in silence.

Finally, Robbie refolded the piece of tapestry and jerkily stuffed it back into his pocket. 'Well, that doesn't make any sense,' he said.

'I'm not sure,' said Layla carefully. '*Destroy the one who comes before* sounds a bit ominous.'

'But who knows what that could mean.' Robbie's voice was a quickfire babble. 'It could mean anything.'

'It sounds like it wants you to . . .'

'Kill my mother?' Robbie laughed a high-pitched laugh. 'I know, ridiculous, right? Obviously, that's not what it means. Otherwise Mother would be dead, wouldn't she, since Brutus pledged *his* heart and everything. Utterly ridiculous.'

Layla bit her lip. 'Robbie, how did Brutus die?'

Robbie was flushed and he didn't know why. 'He d-died in battle,' he said, tripping over his words in the haste to get them out of his mouth. 'Fell out of a castle b-balcony while f-fighting the enemy. Mother's told me the story a thousand times at least.'

Layla looked into Robbie's eyes while Robbie tried to look anywhere else. 'Robbie,' she said gently. 'Are you okay?'

'I'm fine,' squeaked Robbie.

'Because I know that if *I* found a mysterious cloth telling me that to claim my destiny I'd have to kill *my* mum, I'd be . . .'

'*I'm fine!*' Robbie furiously wiped the sweat from his brow and smiled too widely. 'Not felt this good in a long time! Gosh, I could go on a run, I feel positively energized! Shall we get going?'

He leapt to his feet and immediately tripped on his shoes, falling face-first into a tree. He tried to get up, but his billowing cloak snagged in a claw of branches, and no matter how hard he tried he couldn't unpick himself because his hands were shaking – why were his hands shaking?

Layla got up and, after watching him flail for a few sad seconds, helped untangle him. 'Are you sure you don't want to rest here for a moment?' she said as she pulled a twig from his cloak.

'I really think we should get going,' said Robbie, grabbing the Sceptre and slinging it on to his shoulder. At his touch it pulsed bright once again, and

Robbie swallowed. 'Absolutely unrelated, I'm sure,' he said to Layla, who had grimaced at the pulse. 'Anyway, I think we're near to the foot of the mountains. We're actually close!'

'All right, we'll get moving, as long as you're okay.'

Robbie didn't miss the worry that tinged Layla's voice, but he decided to ignore it as they began walking further down the path.

CHAPTER EIGHTEEN

The Queen hadn't spoken for twenty-five minutes. Devon knew it had been exactly twenty-five minutes because she'd been counting the seconds. Robbie and Layla had evaded a third attempt to retrieve the Sceptre, and the Queen hadn't screamed, spoken or even moved since. All she had done for the last twenty-five minutes was stare motionlessly into the orb.

Devon found this much worse than any actual screaming. For the first time in her life, she found herself wishing the Queen would start throwing things again.

'*They knew.*'

Devon jumped as the Queen slowly, ever so slowly, turned around. Her lined face dripped contempt.

'They *knew*. They *knew* that my friend couldn't see – every single thing I have thrown their way, that little cockroach has been one step ahead. *HOW?* Robbie is *NOT THAT SMART!*'

The Queen slammed her fist against the stone bird bath, causing it to crack in two, then crumble into pieces as it hit the ground. Devon squeezed her lips together as hard as she possibly could as the Queen gazed out of the broken aviary window.

'I think they have help.'

Devon's blood turned to frozen slush. She clasped her hands behind her back so tightly they turned purple, as the Queen's eyes drifted slowly back to hers. Her yellow irises locked on to Devon's as she approached her servant, coming so close to her that their noses touched. When the Queen spoke, her voice was barely above a whisper.

'Do *you* know how they've managed to survive this long, Devon?'

It took every ounce of Devon's strength to make

herself shake her head. 'No, my mistress,' she whimpered. 'I've no idea at all.'

The Queen's eyes bored into Devon's a few moments longer, before she finally stepped past her and moved to the door. Devon turned to follow, but the Queen held out a hand.

'No,' she said. 'You stay here and watch the orb. I have one more friend to contact. That little peasant girl thinks she's safe in the trees ... well, let's see how much she enjoys climbing trees after tonight.'

CHAPTER NINETEEN

Robbie had no idea how long they'd been walking, but his feet hurt.

There'd been no sign of another clearing since the tentacle attack, and the darkness was starting to feel oppressive. Even the glow of the Sceptre wasn't enough for comfort. In fact, for Robbie it was the opposite, and its continuous hum was like someone constantly whispering to him in a language he couldn't quite understand. What's more, the hum had become especially loud since he'd read the tapestry. He knew the Sceptre was trying to get his attention, trying to get him to take notice, but every time he listened, the words that filled his head fluttered away as quickly as they'd come.

Another thought was prodding at Robbie as he plodded along the path, and that was the feeling that it was all becoming a little bit *unfair*. He really didn't understand why a Sinistevil such as himself, someone who had no choice but to be born evil, was being told by a silly piece of tapestry to . . . to . . .

Robbie shuddered. He couldn't bear to so much as think the words.

Why would the Sceptre even want him to do . . . what it wanted him to do? Hadn't he proven he was evil enough by stealing the Sceptre and running away in the first place? And now it wanted him to perform another task so unspeakable that Robbie couldn't even consider it. The Sceptre had gone too far.

Robbie looked down at the Sceptre and sniffed. Was there such thing as 'too far' when it came to evil? Mother certainly didn't seem to think so, considering how she ruled Waning. Maybe the Sceptre wasn't being unfair. Maybe Robbie just didn't *want* to do what it wanted him to do.

But what did that mean?

'Robbie?'

Layla was beside him. It was hard to tell in the dim light, but she seemed tired, the bags under her eyes deepened by the hazy green glow. Robbie forced a smile.

'What's up?'

'Do you want to stop for a minute?'

Robbie couldn't think of a better idea in the world. His burst of nervous energy had been well and truly spent, and now all he wanted to do was lie down and sleep for a week.

The pathway had widened greatly to accommodate a particularly large tree, which was monumental in size compared to all the others on the path. It seemed the perfect place for a good rest. Robbie leant back against the tree's massive trunk and slid down to the ground, sighing heavily as he placed the Sceptre on his lap. Layla sat down across from him and yawned.

Robbie smiled.

'What?' said Layla.

'It's just like being back home,' said Robbie. 'At our tree.'

Layla smiled, then her lips sank downwards.

'Is everything okay?' she said. 'You've been awfully quiet for a while now. You've not even talked about Brutus once.'

'I'm fine,' said Robbie. 'Just hungry, I guess. Our lunch got stolen, remember?'

'Are you sure it isn't something else?'

Robbie felt his smile start to slip. He looked down at his lap. There was a lot he wanted to say to Layla, so many things bubbling around in his head it was almost unbearable. He felt the piece of tapestry in his pocket and heard the murmur of faraway words as the Sceptre hummed to him. He wanted to talk about *that*. 'I was just . . .'

Layla nodded encouragingly. Robbie sighed. He couldn't.

'. . . hungry. That's all.'

Layla pursed her lips. Then she looked down at the Sceptre.

'So, um, to be an evil ruler, you need the Sceptre, right? Tell me how it works.'

Robbie took a deep breath and lifted the Sceptre off his lap. 'Well, it takes all the evilness inside you and amplifies it, taking away every inhibition. It knocks down every wall between your conscience and the worst possible thing you could think of doing. Not that I have a conscience.' Robbie cleared his throat. 'No Sinistevils do. Which is why the Sceptre works so well for us, I guess.'

'Okay,' said Layla slowly. 'And what does it do if it's used by someone who, for example, *isn't* evil?'

Robbie raised his eyebrows. 'The Sceptre's been in the Sinistevil family for generations, ever since my ancestors created it. It's never encountered someone who isn't evil. It would never have to.'

Layla chewed her lip. 'So, completely hypothetically, if it *were* to encounter someone with an absolutely un-evil heart, what would happen to that person?'

Robbie shrugged. 'Honestly, I don't know. And I guess we'll never find out. All I do know is that once I pledge my heart, everything will be exactly as it should be.' Robbie frowned, and thought of the piece of tapestry in his pocket. 'At least, I always thought it would be.' He looked back up at Layla. 'What's with all the Sceptre questions?'

'I just wanted to make sure,' Layla mumbled, wrapping her arms around her knees. 'That evil or not, when you pledge your heart you'll still be . . . *Robbie*. Because if not . . . I'll miss you, you know?'

Robbie watched as Layla dug her chin into her knees. Then he sat up straight. 'Of course I'll still be Robbie,' he said. 'How can I be anything else?' He nudged Layla with his foot until she returned his smile, laughing despite herself.

'The only thing different about me will be that I'll finally be making Mother proud . . .' Robbie leant his head back against the tree trunk. His smile started to wobble. 'That's all I really want, you know? I'm her only son and I know I'm not as good as my brother, and I know she'd rather have Brutus ruling than me, but . . . I just don't want her to be disappointed.' He sniffed, then wiped his eyes on his sleeve.

Layla reached out and squeezed his shoulder. 'Robbie Sinistevil, you are going to be an amazing ruler with or without the Sceptre. I don't know what you're worrying about.'

Robbie stretched out his legs and looked up at the branches above them. For a moment, it really did feel as though they were back at home, laughing under their truffle tree. For a moment, everything seemed almost right. He smiled at Layla.

'And you're going to be an amazing Vice Evil Dictator.'

Layla grinned. 'You're really going to make me your official second-in-command?'

Robbie rolled his eyes. 'Layla, you're *already* my official second-in-command. I don't know how many times I'd be dead now if it weren't for you. Besides, who else is going to redesign the entire Sinistevil staff wardrobe?' He held up his hands. 'You know I'm useless at hemming.'

Layla leant over and wrapped Robbie in a hug so tight it rivalled one of his own. 'The castle staff are going to look *so good* when I'm done with them,' she said by his ear. When they separated, however, her smile wavered. 'I was also going to ask you,' she said carefully, not quite meeting Robbie's eye, 'about that rhyme . . .'

Before Robbie could speak, the Sceptre flashed bright, then dimmed them back into near darkness. He cleared his throat. 'I'm sure that's normal,' he said. 'I'm sure that's what it's supposed to do . . .' He shrugged, then sighed. 'Layla, am I being oblivious?'

Layla frowned. 'You're going to have to narrow it down a bit.'

'*Destroy the one who comes before.*' Robbie didn't want to say it, he *really* didn't want to say it, but he could no longer ignore the nagging worry that phrase had brought with it. He looked at Layla, his lip wobbling and his eyes watery. 'Does the Sceptre want me to kill Mother?'

Layla shrugged. 'I think that might be exactly what the Sceptre wants you to do.'

Robbie shook his head. 'It *can't* mean that. It can't! Why on earth – I don't see how – why would Mother . . .' He pulled the tapestry out of his pocket and held it up, shaking it in his balled fist. 'This – this *thing* has to be some sort of a mistake, right? I mean, it *was* ripped off the main tapestry, which probably meant it wasn't supposed to be there in the first place!' Robbie stuttered a few more times before spitting out the words, 'Brutus wielded the Sceptre, and *he* didn't kill Mother!'

'How long did Brutus wield the Sceptre for again?' said Layla.

Robbie chewed his lip hard. 'Half an hour. But I'm absolutely certain those facts are entirely unrelated in any way, shape or form.' He stuffed the tapestry back into his pocket.

'There's something about this situation that we're not quite addressing here,' said Layla, raising an eyebrow. 'You're having such trouble with the concept of killing your mother, but wouldn't that be the most positively *evil* thing you could ever do?'

The Sceptre flashed again, and every cog in Robbie's brain jammed at once. When they finally started whirring again, he opened his mouth – and was interrupted by a buzzing from his pocket. He tried not to act too relieved as he scooped out the orb and held it up. Layla shuffled to his side.

'Devon?' said Robbie; it was difficult to see in the dim light.

'*Master!*' said Devon. '*Listen to me very carefully – how close are you to the Sunken Mountains?*'

'Very close,' said Robbie. 'We should be there by tomorrow morning if we rest tonight.'

'*Do you have a map? Where does it say you are now? This is vitally important!*'

'Um,' said Robbie. 'It kind of got stolen by a load of tentacles . . .'

'*Never mind*,' snapped Devon. '*The Queen has one more friend coming for you, she said they'll be there once the sun has set.*'

'We can't even tell if the sun's set right now!' said Layla. 'The trees are too thick!'

If it was possible, Devon's eyes grew wider. '*You need to get away from the trees. You need to get away from the trees as soon as you can!*'

'That's easy for you to say,' said Robbie. 'We're in a forest. Wait a minute – you said "friend". We haven't met any of Mother's friends yet – only creatures that have been trying to eat us or steal the Sceptre.'

Devon paused, then cleared her throat. '*Master,*' she said carefully, '*surely you must have noticed something about all these creatures, and the fact that they keep appearing whenever your mother says she's sending—*'

'Don't bother,' said Layla. 'I've tried.'

Just as Devon started to reply, another face appeared in the orb. The face loomed silently behind Devon, an ugly smile smeared across its ugly face. Robbie smiled so wide his cheeks nearly split.

'Mother!' he cried. 'How have you been?'

Devon's eyes bulged and she spun around. Then the orb went blank.

Layla snatched the orb from Robbie's hand and shook it. 'Hello? Devon?' She leapt to her feet. 'Oh no. Oh no, oh no, oh no, this is bad! Now we won't know anything about your mother's friend until we meet them ourselves!'

'Hm,' mused Robbie. 'I wonder why Mother didn't stop to say hello? Maybe the signal got lost.'

'Get a grip, Robbie!' snapped Layla. 'Devon's probably not going to survive the night now the Queen knows she's been helping us!'

Robbie's green cheeks paled slightly. 'Why?' he said. 'What's happened to Devon?'

The ground began to quake. Robbie stood up, clasping the Sceptre in both hands. Leaves fell as the forest floor shook, and for a horrible moment he thought the tentacles were back.

That was when he heard the laugh. A deep, rumbling laugh which reverberated throughout the entire forest. Robbie listened, gripping the Sceptre – it was coming from behind him! He turned around and watched as the tree they'd been sitting under began to shake and grow, its roots tearing from the ground as it flexed two enormous arm-like branches. Two holes opened up in its trunk and blinked, revealing eye sockets filled with a bright amber glow which lit up the forest like firelight. The trunk cracked and twisted into a massive grin as the Tree loomed over Robbie and Layla, its stretch crushing all the trees around it.

The Tree bent forwards and grinned.

'ROBBIE SINISTEVIL, I PRESUME? YOUR WONDERFUL MOTHER SENDS HER REGARDS!'

CHAPTER TWENTY

Layla leapt forward and shoved Robbie out of the way as the Tree swung an enormous branch towards them. The Tree only laughed, a booming laugh which shook the earth, as it picked up Layla and flung her backwards like a doll. She screamed as she disappeared into the darkness.

'Layla!' cried Robbie, rushing forward – but something caught his throat and yanked him back. The branch that had snagged his cloak snapped and Robbie stumbled over his shoes, landing in the dirt with a heavy bump.

'AM I HEARING THIS RIGHT?' laughed the Tree, its

voice low and musical. 'A *SINISTEVIL* CALLING OUT
TO A *PEASANT*? OH, THIS IS JUST TOO RICH!'

Robbie looked up into the Tree's jagged smile and
clutched the Sceptre tight. He tried to run around it,
only to be snagged again and sent sprawling backwards into the dirt. He scrambled to his feet.

'Layla! Where are you? Are you all right?' he
cried.

'OH, COME ON, NOW,' boomed the Tree, its amber
eyes shining across Robbie's face. 'I DIDN'T HIT HER
THAT HARD. NOT LIKE *THIS*!'

A branch swung low and swept Robbie's feet from
under him. He hit the ground hard, his chin banging
against the floor with such force it sent his teeth
rattling.

The Tree bent over him as he tried to get back up.
'YOU KNOW, BEATING YOU UP WOULDN'T BE NEARLY
AS EASY IF YOU WERE WEARING CLOTHES THAT
ACTUALLY *FITTED*.' A thin branch came down and
picked at Robbie's sleeve. 'WAIT A MINUTE; ARE
THESE *BRUTUS'* CLOTHES? NOW THAT'S JUST SAD.'

Robbie looked up through watery eyes as he
wobbled to his feet. 'You knew Brutus?'

The Tree straightened. 'ME AND DEAR OLD VIELLA

GO WAAAY BACK. I REMEMBER THAT BAG OF MUSCLES SHE CALLED HER FIRSTBORN. KID COULD'VE CRUSHED ROCKS IN HIS HAND.' The Tree looked Robbie up and down and whistled. 'WHAT HAPPENED TO *YOU*?'

Robbie puffed out his chest. 'Where's Layla?'

'Robbie!' called a voice. 'I'm fine!'

'NOT FOR LONG.' The Tree grinned, and Robbie heard Layla scream. One of its boughs swung forward and Robbie could only watch as Layla was suspended in mid-air, her arms pinned to her sides by a giant wooden fist.

Panic seized Robbie, and he stormed straight up to the face of the Tree. 'Let her go-*agh*!'

The Tree laughed as it flicked Robbie on to his back and squashed him down with a hand-shaped bough.

'I DON'T THINK SO, TINY MAN,' said the Tree. 'I'M RUNNING AN ERRAND FOR AN OLD FRIEND. NOW, HAND OVER THE SCEPTRE AND I'LL CONSIDER DROPPING THIS LITTLE LADY FROM A SURVIVABLE HEIGHT. IF NOT . . .'

The bough pressed down on Robbie's chest and the air rushed from his lungs. He could feel his clockwork heart ticking hard against his ribcage as he gasped for breath, the Sceptre digging painfully into his hands. With what little strength he could manage, he glared up into the Tree's eyes and said, 'I don't think . . . Mother will be too happy . . . if you kill me!'

The Tree lifted its branch and Robbie gasped. He staggered up triumphantly, hugging the Sceptre to himself – until he realized the Tree was laughing again.

'OH, BOY!' cried the Tree, its leaves shaking violently with each guffaw. Then it bent down and brought its gigantic face right up to Robbie's, so close that its bark skinned the tip of Robbie's nose. 'LITTLE BOY, I DON'T THINK YOU KNOW WHAT WOULD MAKE YOUR MOTHER HAPPY AT ALL.'

Robbie swallowed hard. 'I know that she wouldn't want you to take the Sceptre until I've p-pledged m-my heart!' he said, trying to keep the shake from his voice. 'As a Sinistevil, I-I order you to drop my friend and leave us be!'

The bark of the Tree creaked and groaned as its enormous orange eyes narrowed, its gaping mouth contorting into a humourless grin. Robbie tried desperately not to whimper.

'NOW, KID,' said the Tree, its voice a low rumble that Robbie felt in his gut. 'I'M ONLY HERE AS A SPECIAL FAVOUR TO VIELLA SINISTEVIL, SO IT DOESN'T MATTER TO ME WHETHER YOU HAND OVER THAT SCEPTRE ALL NICE AND WILLING, OR WHETHER I PULL IT OUT OF YOUR MANGLED HANDS. BUT SEEING AS YOU'VE GIVEN ME SUCH A HEART-WARMING PLEA, I'M GOING TO BE STRAIGHT WITH YOU. LET ME TELL YOU A FEW THINGS ABOUT YOUR MOTHER.'

A branch caught Robbie's legs and flipped him upside down, dangling him before the Tree's amber eyes. He clung to the Sceptre as the world upturned and his arms fell above his head.

'FIRST OF ALL,' said the Tree, 'YOUR MOTHER DOESN'T *WANT* YOU. SHE DOESN'T EVEN *LIKE* YOU! IN FACT, SHE THINKS YOU'RE THE WORST THING THAT'S EVER BEEN INFLICTED ON HER IN HER ENTIRE LIFE!'

'That's not true!' cried Robbie, his voice cracking.

'OH, I'M LYING, AM I?' laughed the Tree. 'I DON'T THINK SO – I'M ONLY REPEATING WHAT DEAR OLD VIELLA TOLD ME HERSELF WHEN SHE ASKED ME TO

PAY YOU A LITTLE VISIT!'

'What . . .?' Robbie muttered, before he was swung hard into a tree. Pain shot through his back and he cried out, but he still clung to the Sceptre as hard as he could. Somewhere in the distance he could hear Layla screaming his name.

The Tree brought him close again. 'SECOND, YOU WANT TO PLEDGE YOUR HEART? HA! THAT'S THE STUPIDEST THING I'VE EVER HEARD! YOU DON'T EVEN *HAVE* ONE, FOR STARTERS.'

'I'm about to get it back!' cried Robbie.

The Tree grinned wickedly. 'REALLY, NOW? WELL, EVEN IF YOU DID – WHICH YOU WON'T – YOU CAN'T PLEDGE A HEART THAT'S NOT EVIL – AND YOU, KID, ARE THE MOST PUNY, INSIGNIFICANT, *ANTI*-EVIL THING I'VE EVER LAID EYES ON.'

Robbie was swung again, and he heard a *crack* as he collided with another tree, the bark tearing his robes and skinning his shoulder. His palms were slippery with sweat, and he could feel the Sceptre sliding through his grip. His knuckles turned pale green as he gripped as hard as he could.

'But,' he whimpered as the Tree held him close again, 'I'm . . . a Sinistevil . . .'

'A NAME DOESN'T MEAN *SQUAT*, KID!' laughed the Tree as it twirled and swung Robbie playfully between its branches. 'LOOK AT YOURSELF! DO YOU THINK EVIL PEOPLE HAVE *FRIENDS*? DO YOU THINK THEY CARE WHEN OTHER PEOPLE GET HURT? DO YOU THINK THEY *CARE* ABOUT *PEOPLE*? YOU COULDN'T BE EVIL IF YOU TRIED, KID, AND YOUR MOTHER COULDN'T CARE LESS IF YOU CAME BACK HOME AT ALL!'

The Tree held Robbie upside down before its giant amber eyes. Robbie was dazed, tears falling up his forehead as the Tree once again brought the bark of its face right up to his. 'NOW,' it said. 'ENOUGH FUN. MY ARMS ARE GETTING TIRED. WHY DON'T YOU HAND OVER THAT SCEPTRE?'

Robbie sniffed hard as the tears continued to fall. The Tree was lying, it had to be . . . but if it wasn't, then . . .

The Sceptre hummed loudly and new words flitted into Robbie's head.

***Stop crying. Why be sad when we can get* angry?**

Robbie jolted. There was a surge in his grip, like electrical energy shooting up through his arms and into his brain. The jewel of the Sceptre shone, and

Robbie's tears dried up and his jaw muscles twitched. He glared at the Tree, an actual *glare*, as he clenched the Sceptre in his fists.

'You want the Sceptre that much?' he said through gritted teeth. 'Here – *have it*!'

He pulled back the Sceptre and, with every ounce of strength he had left, swung it into the Tree's eye.

'AAAAAAAAAARGH!'

Something shattered as Robbie fell through the air. He landed in a heap on the ground, the Sceptre flying from his hands and bouncing across the dirt. Robbie reached for it before the Tree could snatch it up – the Tree, however, was preoccupied, clutching its eye with its ragged branches and crying out in pain.

'WHAT DID YOU *DO*?' screamed the Tree. 'HOW COULD – HOW DID YOU *DO* THAT?'

It looked down at Robbie, who had already picked himself up and was holding the Sceptre like a sword. Its jewel was pulsing bright.

The Tree snarled. 'YOU WILL *PAY* FOR THAT, YOU TINY LITTLE . . .!' It lifted a giant branch, which curled into a giant fist. Robbie trembled, and as he did the Sceptre shone again, filling the clearing with bright green light. A whimper caught in his throat and stayed there. The muscles in his arms twitched again as once more new words flew into his brain, words that said *Yes, HURT it, teach it a lesson!*

The Tree brought down its branch, and this time Robbie rolled out of the way, avoiding becoming a mushy pile of Sinistevil by mere inches. The Tree slammed its fist over and over again like a demented whack-a-mole, each time missing Robbie as he rolled gracelessly through the dirt. Robbie leapt to his feet, pulled back the gleaming Sceptre and sent it spinning into the Tree's remaining eye. It collided with the bright orange iris, and another loud *SMASH* echoed through the clearing.

The Tree threw back its huge trunk of a body as it howled in pain. It bent down, both eyes closed, and felt about the clearing with a spindly branch.

'HOW,' it groaned, searching for Robbie amid the debris, 'HOW DID YOU . . . BUT VIELLA *TOLD* ME ABOUT YOU – I'VE BEEN WATCHING YOU SINCE YOU CRAWLED INTO THIS FOREST – *YOU* DON'T WANT TO HURT *ANYTHING* . . .'

'*I'm a Sinistevil*,' growled Robbie.

The Tree stopped feeling about and froze. The

Sceptre was humming loudly, *happily*, where it lay glowing on the ground. The Tree turned towards the sound and winced as it heard the loud hum. Finally, it straightened itself, both eyes still glued firmly shut.

'IT SEEMS THAT I HAVE BEEN MISINFORMED,' it said. 'I DON'T KNOW WHAT'S HAPPENING HERE, AND I'M NOT WAITING AROUND TO FIND OUT.'

And with that the Tree turned and fled through the forest, tearing a giant path through the trees as it escaped on its frantic roots.

Robbie looked at the Sceptre where it lay nestled in a groove of upturned earth. It was humming so loudly now, the light of its jewel pulsing off the remaining trees, brighter than it ever had before. It didn't have a single scratch on it.

Robbie had felt something. When he'd wielded the Sceptre and hit the Tree, something had taken over him, something that had felt his emotions and told him what to do. It was as though the Sceptre had broken something inside him.

And everything the Tree had said . . .

'Robbie!'

He turned around as Layla flung herself through

the newly made clearing. She was crying with relief, her arms outstretched. 'Robbie! Are you hurt?'

But Robbie wasn't paying attention.

It was as though someone had gone into his memories and turned on a light. He could hear every conversation he'd ever had with Mother, every single word she had ever said, but something was different. Something had changed.

'Robbie?' Layla was standing in front of him now, her arms dropped. She spoke softly. 'Are you all right?'

'Why would I be all right?' said Robbie. His voice felt disconnected, like it was coming from somewhere far away. 'My mother doesn't want me. She's been trying to get rid of me this whole time. My mother – who always regretted I wasn't Brutus. My mother – who would rather have me dead and in pieces than rule her empire – who traded my own *heart* so I wouldn't get in the way.'

Something stirred in him as he spoke, something deep and heavy that he'd never felt before in his life, filling him up like liquid lead. The Sceptre started whispering again.

Layla went to put her hand on Robbie's shoulder.

'Robbie, I know . . .'

'Of *course* you know!' snapped Robbie, smacking Layla's hand away. 'Because it's so painfully obvious – you've been telling me ever since we started this stupid journey! *Everyone* knew, except poor little Robbie! Puny, stupid Robbie who didn't notice that his mother hated him, because he's too stupid to notice anything – he didn't even notice that he was missing a heart!'

Layla held her hand to her chest, her face a mixture of hurt and confusion.

Robbie didn't care if he'd hurt his friend. He didn't care about anything any more.

A low roll of thunder mumbled over the clearing, and Robbie looked up into the night sky. A deep grey cloud was forming above them.

'Robbie,' said Layla, biting her lip. 'Look, we'll talk about it, okay? It's going to be all right.' She stepped forward again, this time holding her arms out for a hug. Robbie shoved her hard, sending her stumbling backwards over the forest debris. She caught herself before she could fall, her expression turning from shock to anger.

'Hey!' she snapped, balling her fists as she

stormed up to Robbie. 'Don't be so mean!'

'What?' said Robbie. 'Do you think I need you here following me about, pitying me? Well, I don't.' He slowly turned his gaze to the Sceptre, which lay pulsing on the ground. 'Because no one is going to pity me ever again.'

Yes, said the words filling his head, ***that's right. You're so close.***

Layla followed his gaze, then stepped in front of him, blocking his view of the Sceptre. 'What's that supposed to mean, Robbie?' she said as another roll of thunder rumbled overhead.

'It means,' said Robbie darkly, 'that if the world wants evil, that's what they'll get.'

'Robbie, that's not you,' said Layla. 'Look, come on, we're nearly at the Sunken Mountains. Let's just meet this doctorcerer, get your heart back and then we'll...'

'We'll what?' yelled Robbie. 'Live happily ever after? Me and my mother who wants me dead? You leading all your little peasant friends into battle? Get over yourself, Layla!'

Robbie watched as Layla took in a deep, shaky breath. 'As your second-in-command...'

'You're *not* my *anything*,' said Robbie. 'Why don't you just go home? I've had enough of people laughing behind my back.'

Layla clenched her jaw hard, her eyes filling with tears. With an angry cry, she ran past Robbie and disappeared into the forest.

Robbie stood alone as Layla's footsteps echoed into nothingness. A pang of guilt threatened to break through his chest, but was drowned out by another heavy roll of thunder. He looked up. The clouds above him had grown thick and dark, the only light around being the green glow of the Sceptre and the violent flashes that came with each burst of lightning zigzagging across the sky.

A sudden breeze chilled the back of Robbie's neck as he walked towards the Sceptre. This was it, deep in his clockwork heart he knew it: the end. *That's right*, said the words in his head, *there will be no more pity, no more laughing behind your back. After this, no one will dare accuse you of being anything but evil. What do you say?*

Robbie reached down to pick up the Sceptre, to pledge his heart . . .

A crash of thunder overhead made Robbie gasp

and stumble back. He held his chest and noticed his hands were shaking. *All* of him was shaking. He tried to steady his breath. *What am I doing?* he thought. *The Sceptre could kill me!* He looked down at the bright, humming jewel on the ground in front of him, and realized just how close he'd come to being toast.

He tried to stop and think clearly, but the thoughts in his head were running so fast he could barely make sense of them. Worse, he still felt so angry, so upset. Another roll of thunder burst the clouds and heavy rain began to fall. Robbie looked down at the Sceptre and gulped. He knew he needed to find shelter, but the last thing he wanted to do was pick it up. Lightning flashed directly above him and with a groan of despair, he grabbed the Sceptre.

He heard the whispers in his ear immediately, even over the raindrops thudding into the dirt. 'Shut up,' he said as he searched for the path. 'Shut *up*.'

There! The path was just ahead – but the Sceptre was so distracting, its jewel flashing bright even through the rain. Robbie could hardly stand it; he held the rod up as high as he could to keep it as far away from himself as possible. *Almost there*, he thought as he ran, with the Sceptre thrust high above his head. *Almost . . .*

A bolt of lightning struck the Sceptre.

Robbie's body jolted and shook as he was filled with electricity. There was a sensation of cogs bursting apart in his chest, and he suddenly didn't feel quite so angry any more. In fact, he didn't feel anything as the lightning ripped through his body, dropping him to the ground as a charred pile of cloak and limbs.

The Sceptre slipped from his hand and rolled away as everything went black.

CHAPTER TWENTY-ONE

The Queen sighed.

She'd finished tying Devon up and throwing her somewhere dark and nasty, returning just in time to see her friend fleeing in fear through the forest. She didn't see the rest, on account of the fact that she'd smashed the orb.

She thought about screaming, thought about tearing the aviary to smithereens, but then thought better of it. A moment of sitting quietly had led her to an epiphany. In a silence grimmer than an approaching storm cloud, she gathered a few of her biggest, meanest-looking crows and readied the reins

- 219 -

wrapped about their beaks. These were her prized beauties, the only ones of her stock big enough to carry her weight, usually reserved for riding into battle.

The Queen was about to step on to their backs when another clever idea popped into her steel-trap mind. She left the aviary and returned with a large, wriggling hessian sack which she threw over her back with ease.

'Hush, now,' she hissed at the sack, which abruptly stopped wriggling. 'We're going on a little trip.'

As the Queen stepped on to the crows' backs and lifted the reins, she cursed herself for not having come to her grand realization sooner:

If you want something done properly, you have to do it yourself.

Off they flew. The crows rose and fell with each flap of their terrible wings. The Queen clutched their reins as the wind whipped through her wiry hair, and she pulled to make the birds rise higher into the sky as they approached the outskirts of Bleak Forest. With one hand she hitched the now-whimpering sack further on to her shoulder.

It was a lovely day for flying. In the distance, a cluster of storm clouds were dissipating into a clear sky.

CHAPTER TWENTY-TWO

It was still dark.

Robbie looked around at the swirling blackness enveloping his world. He couldn't move. He couldn't feel anything, except a vague cold dampness. Somewhere far away the wind was howling; he could hear it underneath a loud ticking and what sounded like water dripping on to metal.

Was this what being hit by lightning was like?

Ah, thought Robbie, *that's right. I was hit by lightning, wasn't I? Hmm . . .*

He'd always imagined being electrocuted to be a lot more painful than this – this sort of numb, empty darkness. Maybe his eyes had melted. It was entirely possible. Either that or he'd died, which was an equally reasonable assumption. Not too many people survived being hit by lightning. Well, if this was death, it was certainly relaxing.

Robbie decided he'd try speaking.

'Hello?' he said into the abyss.

'Good morning,' answered the abyss in a gruff monotone voice.

Well, thought Robbie, *no one said I* wouldn't *be sharing the afterlife.*

'I assume you think you are dead,' said the abyss.

'I haven't ruled it out,' replied Robbie.

'Have you ruled out opening your eyes?'

Robbie fought against a thick crust of sleep as he prised apart his eyelids.

'Oh,' he said, looking up at the wooden ceiling above him.

'You cannot move,' said the voice, a female voice. 'Do not panic, it is completely normal.'

A soft metallic clinking from just below Robbie's chin drew his attention. He tried to look down, but no matter how hard he strained his neck he remained completely motionless. Somewhere around his abdomen, the gruff voice sighed.

'You say, "You cannot move, do not panic," and the first thing they do is try to move. Why listen to what *I* have to say? I am only the best doctorcerer in the country, but clearly that counts for very little. Stop trying to crane your head, it's distracting.'

Robbie's eyes wandered around the room. He seemed to be in some sort of log cabin. Under the dim light he could see that all sorts of metallic devices and contraptions hung on the walls, none of which he recognized. He listened to what he'd previously assumed were the sounds of the afterlife: the noise of the wind beating against the window and the loud ticking of a wall clock.

'Excuse me,' he said. 'Where am I?' He was aware of how little he could physically feel as he spoke, as though the words were simply drifting from his mouth.

The monotone voice spoke again. 'You are in surgery.'

'Oh,' said Robbie. 'Definitely not dead?'

'I am quite certain of it.' The doctorcerer lowered her voice. 'The dead are usually a lot quieter.'

'Okay,' said Robbie. 'It's just that I don't feel

entirely . . . alive.'

The doctorcerer sighed again, this time harder. 'This is very intricate work I am doing here. It is in both our best interests that you allow me to continue undisturbed.'

'All right,' said Robbie. 'It's just that . . .'

There was a heavy clank like that of a metal instrument being dropped on to a tray in exasperation. A face appeared over Robbie's. It was worn and wrinkled, the reddish-brown skin half obscured by a surgical mask. The person's long blonde hair had been scraped back into a scruffy ponytail, where one or two scalpels were lodged for safe keeping.

'You want proof you are still alive?' said the doctorcerer, reaching behind Robbie's head and tilting it upwards. 'Here you go.'

If Robbie had been able to feel his stomach, he was certain it would have lurched. Nothing was exactly where it should have been; his ribs lay splayed open like a butterfly, revealing the messy organs underneath. The proof of Robbie's life lay in the way his lungs were still expanding and shrinking, despite the fact that he couldn't even feel himself breathing. His stomach churned, and he *heard* it.

'Ugh,' said Robbie.

'I did say you were in surgery,' said the doctorcerer. 'Now, may I return to my work?'

'I think I'm going to be sick.'

'I would advise against it; you are in enough of a mess as it is.'

Robbie felt like everything was floating. How on earth had he got here? He tried to reach his most recent memories. He knew he'd been struck by lightning, but everything around that seemed unbearably foggy. What had he been doing?

He ventured another question. 'Awfully sorry to interrupt – you wouldn't happen to know what happened to me, would you?'

The doctorcerer grunted. 'This was so much easier when you were a baby,' she muttered. 'You did not keep chattering on.'

'Wait, a baby . . . Are you Doctorcerer Clampit?'

'That I am,' said Clampit, pushing another surgical instrument into Robbie's chest. 'Although I doubt you actually remember me. Who would have thought your family would come back to irritate me twelve years on? I hope that Sceptre of yours is worth all the trouble you keep causing me.'

'I've been looking for you!' said Robbie. 'Me and . . . wait, where's Layla?'

'No friends or family allowed in the operating room.'

'She's here?'

'And a good thing she is, too. If she had not dragged you into my surgery when she did, I am fully certain you would be no more than a smouldering pile in the middle of the forest.'

Robbie's misty weightlessness was pierced by an intense warmth, like sunshine bursting through cloud. Layla was okay! Layla was okay, and she'd brought him here; they must have been much closer to the mountains than they'd thought when she'd run off, because . . .

The sunshine was quickly doused with cold, heavy rain as Robbie remembered their argument.

'I can't believe she came back for me,' he muttered. 'After everything I said to her.'

'Mmhmm,' mumbled Clampit.

Robbie stared up at the wooden ceiling. 'Is she all right? I mean, maybe not about me – she must hate me.'

'The young lady is in far better condition than

you were,' said Clampit. 'Only a few cuts and bruises. You, however, resembled overdone toast.'

'Because I was struck by lightning,' said Robbie. 'But why was I struck by lightning? What was I doing? – *ohhh* . . .'

And then Robbie recalled everything in one terrible torrent: the Tree, the anger, and everything else he'd been thinking before he tried to reach for the Sceptre.

'I nearly pledged my heart . . .' he muttered.

'Did you, now,' said Clampit, snipping away at something behind Robbie's lungs.

'I did,' said Robbie. 'Before I was hit, I . . . it was calling to me. It was so loud, and I felt . . .' He blinked. 'What would have happened, Doctorcerer? If I *had* actually . . .'

Clampit slammed down her instruments in frustration and wheeled back into Robbie's field of vision. 'Well,' she snapped. 'It would have been just one of the many ways you planned on melting the perfectly good heart I gave you, wouldn't it? Look at it now – a piece of world-class engineering reduced to a clockwork blob.'

'I'm very sorry,' said Robbie. 'But if my heart

melted, why am I not dead?'

'I am very talented,' said Clampit.

'Oh,' muttered Robbie as Clampit returned to the surgery. 'Um . . . thank you. Are you putting in a new one?'

'Your friend made the suggestion of your *old* one.'

Robbie gasped. 'You still have it?'

'Yes,' grunted Clampit. 'As it was used in an act of magic, it would have been irresponsible to throw it away. However, I suggest you take better care of this one. Hearts don't grow on trees, you know.'

'I'll look after it, I promise!' said Robbie. 'I'll pledge it and—' He stopped and gazed at the ceiling. There was another thought knocking around his head, one that disconcerted him. He had wanted to pledge his heart, the thing he'd been working towards his whole life, and at the last minute he'd backed out, and it had left him feeling . . .

Relieved?

And not just because he would have died, either.

'I think I might have hated,' he said quietly. 'I felt it – when I wanted to pledge my heart.'

'I imagine you did,' said Clampit. 'And did it stick?'

'No . . .' said Robbie. 'I don't think it did.'

'Do you feel evil?'

'Not particularly.'

'Mr Sinistevil, do you even *want* to be evil?'

Robbie listened to the wind outside, rattling the windows of the log cabin, while the wall clock ticked on. 'No,' he said eventually. 'No, I don't. I know I only did it a tiny bit before, but . . . Doctorcerer, I don't think I ever want to feel like that again.'

Doctorcerer Clampit returned her attention to Robbie's chest cavity. 'I believe some people are simply not wired that way. This is not a bad thing.'

'To think,' Robbie muttered. 'That's how Brutus felt *all the time* . . . oh, but wait a minute.' He tried to look at Clampit again. 'What if it happens again? What if the Sceptre calls me and I have to feel that way again?'

'Everyone gets taken over by their feelings from time to time. Now, where did I put . . . ah, here it is.'

Robbie could hear Clampit rummaging through a box underneath the operating table. There was a slow creak, as though the lid she was lifting hadn't been touched in many years. 'You never forget a heart,' she said. 'It is a little small at the moment, but once it is in, it will grow to size. Do not be alarmed if it feels loose at first. Now, you may experience a tingling sensation . . .'

Robbie heard a deep squelching noise from somewhere around his chest, and then a feeling of pure light flooded through his veins.

'Is that my heart?' he whispered.

'It is indeed,' muttered Clampit. 'You still need stitching up, but I believe the surgery has been a complete success. Now, get some sleep. It sounds as though you owe your friend a long, uncomfortable conversation.'

Robbie closed his eyes and disappeared back into the misty darkness.

CHAPTER TWENTY-THREE

Robbie was awoken by a sunbeam moving across his face. He opened his eyes, then winced at the brightness and squeezed them shut again. The grey clouds from the morning still hung around the sky, but a few rays of dim sunlight managed to struggle through the dusty window of the surgery and washed over Robbie, warming him. The surgery was eerily quiet without the wind and rain spitting at the glass. The wall clock was left to pick up the slack, ticking ever louder until Robbie could no longer ignore it.

He decided it was probably time to get up.

He experimented, first wiggling his fingers, then his toes. They all seemed to be in working order. Next, he tried his arms; they were stiff, and his back ached from the hard surface of the operating table, but he could move at least. He bent his elbows and leant forward.

His groggy head swam as he sat up, and a deep ache travelled up his chest. He groaned and tried to keep from swaying. Something wasn't quite right; the ache in his chest felt different to anything he'd felt before, almost like there was something trapped behind his ribcage trying to gently wriggle free. He looked down at the deep red line travelling from the top of his chest to his abdomen, and ran a finger over the bumps of the black stitches holding him together. *Clampit must have used some magic*, he thought, *these stitches are nearly fully healed*.

Then, with a quivering hand, he placed his palm against his chest.

There it was, a low *ba-bump, ba-bump*. His heart. It felt so odd, so *alive*. He wondered if he'd ever get used to it.

It struck Robbie that he'd just woken up into a world that was entirely different and new. Everything he'd ever known had been blasted into ash by the lightning strike. What was he supposed to do now? He took a deep breath and decided to run through his options. Firstly, what had changed? Well, he had a human heart now, that was one thing. He'd also figured out that he wasn't evil, that he didn't want to pledge his heart, and that his mother hated him and wanted him gone – ideally dead, if the Sceptre would allow it. So where did that leave him? What *were* his options? *Well*, he thought, *I can always . . .*

He bit his lip and furrowed his brow.

I could become a farmer? Or a peasant, a secret peasant so that Mother doesn't find me. Or . . . Robbie sighed and slumped forwards so that his elbows dug into his knees. *Or I could become someone with absolutely no purpose in the world. Yes, that seems about right.*

There was a knock at the door.

'Come in,' called Robbie, before he realized. 'Wait! I'm topless!'

A head peeked round the door, a head with big, tight black curls. Thankfully, the person had one hand over her eyes. 'It's me,' said Layla. 'I've got your clothes. Can I come in? I won't look.' She had a bag over her shoulder, and was balancing a set of neatly folded black robes in her free hand.

Robbie jumped from the operating table, snatched up his robes and whipped them on. 'Okay,' he said, climbing back on to the table. 'You can look now.'

Layla closed the door and opened her eyes. 'Are they all right?'

Robbie looked down at his clothes and realized that his elbow no longer stuck out of the giant claw marks the rat had made, and even the lightning scorches looked remarkably neat. He looked back up at Layla, who stood in the middle of the room, clasping her hands together and shuffling her feet.

'I know you didn't want anyone altering Brutus' robes,' she said nervously. 'But I thought that maybe he wouldn't mind them being neatened up a bit. Also, I didn't have a lot to do while you were in surgery, so . . .'

Robbie tried to speak, but didn't know what to say. He stared at Layla as he tried to work it out. Layla's patchwork overalls had held up better than Robbie's robes, but her arm was wrapped in a clean white bandage. Layla followed his eyes and shrugged.

'It's just from where that tree dropped me,' she said. 'But Doctorcerer Clampit is very good, I can barely feel it now. So . . . how are *you* feeling?'

Robbie sighed. 'Stupid and mean.'

Layla sat down next to him. 'I meant after your surgery, but yeah, that too, I guess. Just so you know, you owe me a *massive* apology.' She kicked her feet as she spoke.

They both sat in silence, listening to the tick of the wall clock. Robbie wrung his hands nervously. Finally, he managed to find the words he wanted to say.

'You came back for me.' He glanced at Layla, who was still staring at her feet. He swallowed. 'I don't know why you did – I completely didn't deserve it. Not after what I said, or how I pushed you, or . . . And none of those things I said were true, you know, I didn't mean a single word of it. I know that doesn't make it any better, and I'm still awful for having done what I did, but . . .' His nose twitched and his chin trembled. 'You're my second-in-command.'

Thick tears ran down Robbie's chin and dripped heavily on to his knees. He dragged his sleeve across his face, leaving a pattern of snot and tears along the arm of his robes. That was when Layla punched him softly on the shoulder.

Robbie glanced up through his tears. He could just about make out the wobbly shape of Layla's smile.

'Apology accepted,' she said, before wiping her eyes with the back of her hand. 'Wow, you're an absolute state, you know that? Your hair is exactly the same, though.' She sniffed. 'You really scared me, you know.'

'When you found me unconscious?' said Robbie.

'No,' said Layla. 'When you were saying all that stuff, before I ran away . . .' She looked back down at her feet.

'Yeah, I understand,' said Robbie sadly. Then he frowned. 'Wait, where's the Sceptre?'

Layla glanced at him nervously.

'I don't want it,' said Robbie quickly. 'I felt its power and it's not for me. I just don't think it should fall into the wrong hands.'

Layla's expression didn't change, but she swung the bag over her shoulder and pulled out the Sceptre. It was completely untarnished, the silver metal gleaming against the jewel's green glow. Robbie felt queasy.

'So,' he said, 'at least we know it's durable.'

He reached out, and Layla pulled it away. 'Sorry,' she said. 'It's just ... Well, the last time you had it you kind of became ...'

'A smouldering mess?' said Robbie.

'I was going to say a massive jerk, but yeah, that too.'

Robbie looked down at the jewel. It was glowing softly, and still humming, but not nearly as loudly as it had been before. Slowly, he hovered his hands over the metal rod. Then he took it.

Immediately, the hum grew loud as a pulse of energy surged up Robbie's arm. He winced, sickened by the feeling, as more words filled his head.

Ready to pick up where we left off?

For a moment, a single horrible moment, Robbie felt all the anger from the night before welling up inside him. He thought of Mother, of everything she'd ever said and ...

He shook his head, nearly losing his grip on the Sceptre. He grabbed it quickly, and the jewel fell close to his chest.

Zap.

A spark. Robbie jumped, and the jewel pulsed once. *Oh no*, he thought.

Layla frowned as she read his face. 'What?' she said.

'I think . . .' said Robbie slowly. What was he supposed to say? He looked into Layla's anxious eyes and considered making up some lie, that the Sceptre was just on the blink or something . . . then he sighed. He couldn't lie. He wasn't evil enough to lie.

'It knows I've got my heart back. And I don't think it's quite done with me yet.' The Sceptre hummed in response.

Layla bit her lip as her eyebrows knitted. 'You don't?'

'I don't.' Robbie looked down at the gently pulsing jewel, before sticking his nose in the air snootily. 'Which is an awful shame, because *I'm* entirely done with *it*.' He put the Sceptre down next to him, trying to hide from Layla how relieved he was to have it out of his hands.

Layla narrowed her eyes. 'Does this mean . . . that you don't want to be evil any more?'

Robbie shook his head. 'Nope. I don't think I do. Being evil is highly overrated, if you ask me.' He rolled the Sceptre towards Layla. 'I just want to be Robbie.'

Layla shook her head. 'But what about pledging your heart?'

'What *about* it?' said Robbie anxiously.

'Don't you have to pledge your heart to be King? And if you're not King, how can you help me fix Waning?'

Robbie blinked slowly as he thought this over. 'Maybe I don't have to pledge my heart to be King,' he said slowly. 'Maybe I can just . . . *be King*. And one of my first decrees will be to get rid of *this* piece of junk once and for all.' He huffed at the Sceptre, which pulsed in response, and his stomach dropped. 'Except I'm not going to be King, because I can't go home. Because of Mother. She's probably going to try and get rid of me the moment I step inside the castle.'

Layla smiled sadly, then pushed the Sceptre back towards Robbie. 'Then I guess we just focus on making sure the Queen doesn't ever get this back. That's why I think you should keep hold of it. I reckon as long as *you* have it, it'll never fall into the wrong hands.'

I'm not so sure about that, thought Robbie as the Sceptre pulsed brightly. 'Maybe we can find a way to break it?' he said. 'Maybe then, Mother will stop trying to kill everyone, and I can go back to trying to be King?'

Layla nodded. 'It's worth a shot. We just need to figure out how.'

The sun beamed through the window one last time before disappearing behind light grey clouds. It began to rain, and Robbie watched the drops streak the glass.

'Mother hates me, Layla.'

'I know that, Robbie.'

He got up and walked to the window. 'It'll be weird, not going home. I wonder what she'll do with my room? And poor Devon, she'll be stuck—'

They both turned to each other, eyes wide, and gasped, '*Devon!*'

'The Queen caught her trying to help us,' said Layla as she began to pace. 'Who knows what could have already happened to her!'

'What can we do?' said Robbie, running back to the operating table.

'Well, we've been fighting all sorts of monsters in the forest,' said Layla. 'What's one monster more? Scratch that last plan – we need to go back to the castle *now*, to save Devon by – by throwing the Queen in the dungeon or something!'

Robbie bit down hard on his lip. His eyes grew shiny as he ran his hands through his hair. 'I don't think I *can* do that to Mother, Layla,' he muttered, falling back on to the operating table. 'She's still . . . she's still . . .'

'Still what?' snapped Layla.

'*She's still my mother!*' wailed Robbie. He slammed his face into his hands. 'Oh, Devon,' he moaned through his fingers. 'Devon, I'm sorry, I'm so confused . . .'

'I thought I warned you not to overexcite my patient.'

Robbie jumped at the gruff voice of Doctorcerer Clampit as she strode into the room. She closed the door behind her and crossed her arms. 'Look at him – he is in a state of complete distress. This is not good for someone recovering from heart surgery, you know.'

'Om frmf ssin trmble,' said Robbie through his fingers.

'What?' said Clampit.

'Our friend is in trouble,' said Layla. 'In Robbie's

castle. His mother has our friend, and we think she's going to hurt them.'

'Well,' said Clampit, turning to Robbie, 'go and tell her to stop.'

Robbie's hands fell to his lap as he gaped at Clampit. 'I can't do that!'

'Why not?' said Clampit.

'Because it's her castle! She can do what she wants, she's reigning there.'

'I thought you were twelve.'

'I am.'

'And someone unsuitable is on your throne?'

'Well, I wouldn't say *unsuitable*, her business ethic wields incredible results . . .'

'*Robbie*,' Layla warned.

Robbie sighed and closed his eyes. 'Yes.'

Clampit picked something out of her teeth. 'If someone unsuitable is on your throne, go and knock them off it. It is *your* throne, is it not?'

The Sceptre hummed, and Robbie heard it whisper: ***Knocking her off your throne is exactly what you should do – in fact, you could knock her off the castle roof while you're at it . . .***

No, thought Robbie. He opened his eyes. Both

– 243 –

Clampit and Layla were now staring at him, and he didn't like it. It all seemed so simple to them, so cut and dried...

'We'd never make it to the castle in time,' muttered Robbie. 'We're all the way on the other side of the forest.'

Clampit rolled her bright green eyes. 'Then you had better get a move on, hadn't you?'

Chapter Twenty-Four

Stepping out into the sharp mountain air was like stepping into another world after the gloominess of Clampit's surgery. The struggling sun turned the sky above bright grey, and Robbie's boots squelched on the tufts of damp grass which exploded from cracks in the rock.

'Huh,' said Layla, looking up at the sky. 'It's stopped raining. That's good.'

Robbie pulled his cloak around him as a chill gust blew around the cliffs. All around him was grey, from the varied streaks of cliffside to the solid off-white of the newly emptied sky. A few feet in front of him, the ground fell in a steep decline. A ragged path wound itself down the side of the mountain, leading directly into the thick, deep-green expanse of Bleak Forest. Robbie noticed a groove in the dirt, leading straight to Clampit's door.

'That's where I dragged you,' said Layla proudly. '*I* should be leading your army. I mean, I won't really – I'm actually thinking of disbanding it.' She winked at Robbie. 'It's on my list.'

'If I become King without dying in the process, I will most certainly support your request,' said Robbie.

Layla raised an eyebrow and laughed. 'Won't your mother be pleased?'

Robbie felt ill. 'Please don't mention Mother.'

Layla smiled sympathetically, and Robbie felt the gentle buzz of the Sceptre in his hand. *Don't think about Mother*, he thought as the Sceptre began to glow brighter, *don't think about her, or any of the things she's done to you,* **or all the ways she should be punished** . . .

Robbie shook his head hard.

'You all right?' said Layla.

'I'm *fine*,' snapped Robbie. Layla stepped back,

and Robbie instantly felt awful. 'Sorry,' he said glumly. Layla nodded, but said nothing.

Robbie was about to apologize again when a single black feather spun gently before his nose. *Huh*, he thought, but then he noticed that Layla was looking just above his head. She opened her mouth to shout, but Robbie didn't hear her. Her voice was drowned out by a deafening—

CAW!

Something sharp gripped his shoulders, and Robbie was hauled into the air. Another loud squawk filled his ears, and Robbie looked up – and decided that he never wanted to see another crow in his life.

Layla sprinted over and leapt, catching Robbie's feet and dangling as she anchored him back to the earth. The crow squawked in protest, and both Robbie and it dipped, its flight wavering as Layla pulled . . .

Thump.

Even with the laces knotted twelve times, Robbie's shoes were still seven sizes too big. He cried out as they slipped from his feet. Layla fell back into the dirt, holding the oversized boots and watching with despair as Robbie disappeared further and further up the jagged heights of the Sunken Mountains.

Robbie clutched the Sceptre close and frantically hoped he was being flown somewhere nice. But suddenly the grip on his shoulder disappeared and he was falling fast, hitting the ground before he could even scream. He opened his eyes and looked around; he was on a large flat plain of smoke-grey stone. He could no longer see the forest beyond the mountains; he was so high up that the view showed only vast sky and a misty layer of cloud below. *Well*, he thought, *at least I wasn't dropped* off *the mountain.*

Robbie stretched out his legs – then gasped as he nearly slid into nothingness. The crow had placed him right at the edge of the cliff, so close that one wrong move on the slippery rock and that was it. Robbie struggled to his hands and knees, pinning the Sceptre to the ground with his palm. He looked up, and froze.

On the other side of the flat expanse, still and silent as a gravestone, was Mother.

The crow cawed loudly as it landed behind her, joining its brother in flanking a large hessian sack which Robbie barely registered; he was too distracted by the sharp yellow eyes piercing him from across the way. There was at least ten feet between them, but Robbie could still feel the bitter cold radiating from Mother. He'd seen her angry before (in fact, he'd rarely seen Mother anything *else* before), but this was different. The anger on Mother's face now was the kind that meant to get results.

'Hello, Robbie.'

Robbie, still on his hands and knees, gulped. 'Hello, Mother.'

He listened out for Layla, but heard nothing. She must be so far away, and so totally unable to save him. At that moment, Robbie's entire world consisted of only himself and Mother.

Mother began to walk towards Robbie. She moved slowly, unbearably slowly, each footstep clacking on the rock like a scythe chipping away at stone.

'So,' she said. 'Off to get your heart back, are you?'

'Um . . .' said Robbie as each of his senses

abandoned him one by one.

'Disobeying my orders? Attacking all my friends? You *are* in a rush to take your place on the throne, aren't you?' She looked Robbie up and down and grimaced, before turning back to her crows. 'It's a good thing we caught you when we did, isn't it? Just as you managed to find Clampit's surgery. Part of me thought you may actually succeed in getting your heart back.' She glared back at Robbie. 'I don't know why I was so worried.'

Robbie frowned, then quickly understood: she didn't know she was too late. Fortunately, the painful dryness in his throat meant he couldn't have corrected her even if he had wanted to.

Robbie could no longer feel his arms and legs, but as Mother made it halfway across the plain he instinctively closed his hand around the Sceptre. Mother noticed, and stopped.

'Get up, you disgusting little worm.'

Without thinking, Robbie stood up straight and awaited further orders. He scolded himself for the reflex; this was *not* the way a rebel typically confronted an evil ruler. He swallowed hard.

'Where's Devon?'

Mother scoffed. 'Oh, I wouldn't worry about Devon. She's perfectly safe for now. *My* turn for a question. Are you ready to give back the Sceptre?'

Robbie flinched at the word and hugged the Sceptre close to his chest, feeling a distinct thrum of energy travel through his cloak. The Sceptre began to hum gently. *No*, thought Robbie despairingly, *not now.*

Mother narrowed her eyes and peered around the cliffs. 'Where's your little friend?' she said. 'The one who's been undertaking the pitiful task of keeping you alive? She hasn't perished in the forest, has she?'

'No,' said Robbie, glancing about with waning hope.

'Shame.' Then Mother's face lit up. 'Well, not to worry! I know how much you like your friends, so I brought one with me just in case.' She turned around and strode back to the crows, reaching for the hessian sack they were diligently guarding. She looked over her shoulder and grinned a sickening grin. 'Wouldn't want you to feel lonely, now, would we?'

She opened the sack and Robbie's stomach lurched. Like a ventriloquist pulling a dummy from its trunk, Mother reached into the sack and yanked out the scruffy figure of Devon. Her usually immaculately neat uniform was rumpled and askew, her hands were bound, and her lip was wobbling.

Eventually she noticed Robbie. 'Hello, Robbie,' she squeaked.

'Hello, Devon,' said Robbie sadly. 'I'm glad you're all right.'

'*All right* might be a b-bit of an overstatement, m-master,' said Devon through chattering teeth.

'I thought,' said Mother, waving Devon about emphatically as she spoke, 'that seeing as how you *love* disobeying me, you may need a little incentive if you were ever to start listening to your dear old mother again.' She dragged Devon forward, and Robbie rushed to meet them, to grab Devon from Mother's grip, but Mother held up a finger that made him freeze in his tracks. 'Ah, ah, ah!' she said, wagging her finger as she pulled Devon along. Finally, they stopped – right at the edge of the cliff.

Mother turned to Robbie, one talon holding a violently quaking Devon mere inches from the sheer cliff edge.

'I'll give you a choice. You get to keep the Sceptre, or Devon. The throne or *friendship*, which one will it be?' She lifted a hand to inspect a nail. 'You have five seconds.'

Robbie clutched the Sceptre as his chin trembled. There was no way he could let Devon fall. Mother had beaten him before he'd even made a move.

'I don't suppose, Devon,' called Robbie, 'that you can see if it's a long way down?'

Devon's eyes widened. 'I don't need to look, master, to know that the drop is *exceedingly* long, so whenever you're ready to make a decision . . .'

Mother's eyes narrowed.

'Five . . .' she began to count down.

Robbie groaned mournfully as he walked towards Mother, Sceptre outstretched. Mother's sick grin grew larger, her slimy black tongue licking her lips as Robbie approached sullenly, his shoulders hunched and his chin on his chest. She held out her free hand.

When Robbie was close enough, he looked up into Devon's tear-filled eyes. 'Thank you,' she whispered. Robbie smiled as wide as he could, which wasn't very, as he held out the Sceptre. Mother's hand twitched with anticipation, then like a spider snatching its prey she grabbed it.

Hummmmmmm.

Robbie bent forwards as a surge of energy shot up his arm. The Sceptre's jewel glowed bright, and Robbie's hands tightened around the rod. Mother looked up, her smile melting downwards.

'Give me the Sceptre, you little slug,' she growled.

But Robbie didn't. He wanted to, he desperately wanted to let go, but something else was inside his head, something familiar which whispered over and over again how easy it would be to *push her, just one nudge and she'll be out of your life for ever, and the kingdom will be yours, all yours, just push . . .*

'Robbie!'

Robbie's head snapped up as two arms reached from the cliff edge behind Mother. A figure hauled itself up on to the rocks – Layla!

The hum of the Sceptre grew quiet as Robbie felt his chest fill with warmth, a warmth which made the whispers disappear in an instant. His smile was genuine now, and it grew the entire width of his face.

Mother took one look at this smile and gagged. She followed Robbie's gaze to Layla, who was now struggling to her feet. Mother scowled a horrifying scowl. Then, flashing a sinister grin back at Robbie, she flung Devon behind her.

'*NO!*'

Robbie yanked the Sceptre out of Mother's claw-ing grasp, sending it clanking across the stone behind him as he ran for his friends. But he couldn't run fast enough without his shoes – Devon slammed into Layla and both started to teeter towards the cliff edge, just as Robbie reached out his arms.

Layla grabbed his hand, and then reached back and caught Devon just as she was about to disappear into the mists below. Robbie pulled Layla, Layla pulled Devon, and then the three fell back hard on to the safety of solid ground.

They all gasped with relief as Robbie and Layla untied Devon's hands, but the relief was short-lived as Robbie remembered—

'The Sceptre!'

There it was, rolling towards them, with Mother not far behind it. Robbie dived on to his belly and caught it, before climbing shakily to his feet – just in time for Mother to lunge.

'You little insect!!'

Robbie wasn't quick enough to dodge the swipe that sent him reeling to the side, spinning him further away from the edge of the cliff. Mother grabbed at the Sceptre, but Robbie fell backwards and pushed himself away with his foot. She was on him in a flash, looming over him with claws outstretched.

Robbie swung the Sceptre at her, but she only grabbed it and kicked him hard in the face. His head snapped back, his vision blurred by tears as the Sceptre left his hands and slipped from Mother's, once again flying back across the rocks.

He sat up and tried to get his bearings. Across the clifftop he could see Mother's crows attacking Devon and Layla, who were frantically swatting at the squawking demons.

Robbie wished he could run to help them, but he needed to get the Sceptre! He scrambled to his feet and shot forwards, slamming right back on to his face. He spat out pieces of stone as he untangled his feet from his billowing cloak.

'Layla!' he cried as he balled up the mass of fabric and threw it across to her. She caught it and immediately used it to snare one of the now furious crows.

Robbie didn't have time to stop and watch: he could see the Sceptre rolling towards the cliff edge!

He raced across the rock, going, 'Ow, ow, ow,'

each time his feet hit the cold stone. Finally, he reached the Sceptre – just as Mother grabbed him by the collar of his shirt, swung him around and shoved him backwards.

There was a horrible rush of cold on the back of Robbie's head. He gripped Mother's wrist for dear life, looking over his shoulder just as the wind blew aside a patch of mist to reveal one hundred feet of nothingness, culminating in some very solid-looking rocks.

He knew that Mother had him suspended, that if she were to let go of his shirt collar that would be it. No more Robbie. He gripped her wrist tighter.

In her free hand Mother held the Sceptre. She gazed into Robbie's terrified eyes and smiled, baring her wicked black fangs. Her mouth opened, but no words came out.

Mother's smile dropped as her eyes went down to the hand grasping Robbie's shirt. It was the hand that could feel his pulse in his neck. She looked back up at Robbie, momentary panic on her face, which quickly turned to furious hatred.

'You little *slug*,' she spat. 'You got your heart back, didn't you?'

Robbie gave her a wobbly grin. 'I knew you'd be happy.'

'All I have to do is let go,' she snarled, 'and you're finally out of the picture.'

'You're not allowed,' said Robbie quickly. 'I know about the rules of the Sceptre! You can't kill me or you'll lose all the Sceptre's power.'

'Ugh,' said Mother. 'Why do you have to pick *now* to start being clever?'

Robbie whimpered as another gust of wind blew by, then locked his eyes on to hers. 'I also know about the final rule.'

Mother's face went through an entire spectrum of emotion, which Robbie would have found fascinating to watch had her face not been quite so close to his. 'You . . . *how*? I hid the . . .' Her features twisted into surprise, confusion, then finally settled on rage. Robbie used her momentary mind-malfunction to kick his right leg upwards, dislodging the Sceptre from Mother's grip and catching it in his hand.

Mother panicked and flung him back on to solid ground. With a roar that shook the Sunken Mountains, she cried: '*This was so much easier with your brother!*'

The clifftop was plunged into a silence broken only by the breeze skating along the rocks. The crows had caught Layla and Devon in their talons and were now gripping them in place. Robbie stared at Mother, whose shoulders rose and fell with each angry breath. His shoeless feet had gone numb with cold, but he barely noticed. His limp arms held the Sceptre low.

He blinked a long, slow blink. 'A Sinistevil has to kill their predecessor before they can fully wield the Sceptre, right?'

Mother stayed by the cliff edge, her hair undulating in the breeze like spiky black tentacles. 'Took you long enough to figure it out.'

Robbie felt his knees shaking. He tried to stand steadily, but it didn't work. When he spoke, he found the shake had spread to his voice. 'S-so, Brutus came to k-kill you?'

Mother made a show of wiping a tear from her eye. 'My own pride and joy. It was heart-breaking.'

'You said he died in glorious battle,' said Robbie.

'He *did* die in glorious battle.' Mother grinned. 'With me.'

Robbie's heart dropped. It was a feeling he was

very much unaccustomed to. He was also unaccustomed to how heavily a real heart *beat*, how hard it managed to struggle against his rib cage. It was making him want to throw up.

In his hand, the Sceptre hummed louder.

Robbie's throat hurt as he spoke. 'But . . . but you can't *do* that – you – you . . . It's against the rules!'

'I *know*,' spat Mother, lurching forward. 'You think I'd still have the Sceptre's power if I'd dispatched of your brother myself? Of *course* I didn't. He found me on the highest balcony of Sinistevil Castle and tried to rush me.' She sniffed. 'I simply stepped out of the way.'

The Sceptre's jewel flashed so brightly it stung Robbie's eyes, but tears were already streaming down his cheeks. When he opened his eyes again he noticed the storm clouds growing in the distance. He tried to concentrate, tried to think of something else – *anything* else – but the only thought that his mind would allow him was Brutus. His big brother, whose death had been a lie. A lie told by Mother. He sniffed hard and tried to stop crying, but he couldn't. He'd never had the big brother he'd always wanted because of *Mother*.

So she deserves to be punished.

The words slipped into Robbie's mind and stayed there, bouncing off every corner of his brain. His tears began to dry.

She hurt you. She's hurt all of your friends, just because she could. She even hurt your brother.

Finish the pact. Take her down. She deserves it.

Yes, thought Robbie. *She does.*

Robbie's grip on the Sceptre grew tighter and tighter, the glow of the jewel growing stronger and stronger. He saw Mother standing across the plain, the confidence in her face slowly ebbing away as the storm clouds overhead crept ever closer.

Ready? said the voice in Robbie's head.

He closed his eyes. *Yes*, he thought, *I'm ready.*

And with that thought, he pledged his heart.

Surges of energy pulsed up Robbie's arms. He felt the power pour through him and mix in his veins. Feelings flooded him, feelings he'd never felt before, washing through every part of him and filling his lungs like air. Even though it was only slightly familiar, Robbie knew the feeling right away:

Hate.

So much hate.

He hated Mother for everything she'd done, hated his brother for stealing all her love. He hated Layla for having a family who loved her, hated Devon for keeping Mother's secrets from him, and he hated every servant in Sinistevil Castle for letting Mother hurt him the way she had. He hated every little thing, and every little ounce of hatred fuelled him. He felt the Sceptre transforming him, empowering him with this almighty, all-encompassing hatred.

Robbie had never hated before.

It felt good.

The Sceptre's jewel gleamed as Robbie drank in the hatred flowing through him. Why had he ever found hating difficult before? This was fun, it was wonderful, it made him feel like the most powerful being in the entire kingdom—

Not yet. Robbie felt the words in his head. *You still have one more thing to do.*

That's right, thought Robbie, and he grinned as he gazed across the clifftop. *I do.* Mother was going to pay for how she'd treated him. He could see her face from where he stood, now well and truly full of regret as she started to edge slowly backwards.

'You wouldn't dare . . .' she croaked.

'*I would!*' Robbie began to walk towards her.

Somewhere to his right he could hear Layla calling him, but she was so easy to ignore now that he had more *fun* things on his mind. The idea of hurting someone, of causing pain to those who'd been laughing at him for so long – it was glorious, energizing, and so very easy.

Claws of lightning tore through the sky, and Robbie stopped and thrust the Sceptre high above his head. The thunder overhead grew deafening. Lightning flashed, and in the chaos Robbie knew he was evil – he knew it, he felt it, *he was evil*! He laughed into the sky, a new laugh, an *evil* laugh. He was finally a Sinistevil—

Beneath Mother's feet, the cliff began to break away. He saw it first in her face – the terror as the ground disappeared beneath her feet. Then *she* disappeared.

Robbie's eyes widened, and the evil smile dropped from his face. He felt the cold wind rush through his hair as he leapt forward.

'Mother!' he cried.

He leant over the edge of the cliff – there she was,

clinging to a rock, her dangling body swaying in the storm. Her nails dug into the cliffside, but Robbie could already hear the rocks cracking. Through the mist of panic he realized that there were now two voices in his head, one laughing gleefully and another quieter one, calling to be heard.

Help her! squeaked the smaller voice, and Robbie realized it sounded very much like his own.

He dropped to his knees and lowered the Sceptre.

'Quick!' he yelled over the wind. 'Grab this!'

'What are you doing?' Mother cried.

What are you doing? echoed the Sceptre in his head. *Let her fall! This is your doing, this is your chance!*

Robbie squeezed his eyes closed and tried to concentrate, but the words just wouldn't stop. *Kick her hand! Push her! Think of what she's done to you, think of all the things she's said! She doesn't deserve the throne, YOU do! LET HER FALL!*

'SHUT UP!' yelled Robbie, before opening his eyes and thrusting the Sceptre downwards. 'Grab it! Quick!'

Mother looked horrified. 'I don't understand,' she said. 'Why are you . . .?'

'I can't let you fall!' said Robbie, tears rolling down his cheeks and dripping from the tip of his nose.

Mother's mouth fell open, but she didn't waste time. She closed her hands around the Sceptre's jewel.

The Sceptre protested. It flashed and buzzed in Robbie's hands as he leant back, arms shaking under Mother's weight. It took all of Robbie's strength to haul her up, and even more to ignore the Sceptre screaming *NO, NO, NO!* in his head as he did. Finally, Mother clambered back on to the clifftop, and both she and Robbie collapsed in a raggedy heap on the ground.

The Sceptre fell silent.

Robbie was shaking as he pulled himself to his feet. He sighed a deep, deep sigh, and as he did all the tension in his muscles melted down his arms and back into the Sceptre. With a gust of wind, the gathering storm clouds dissipated completely. He could no longer hear humming, and when he looked down at the Sceptre it wasn't glowing any more. In fact, for the first time since Robbie had touched it, it felt completely inanimate. He shook it once or twice to make sure, to be certain there were no more surprises.

The Sceptre stayed quiet, and Robbie knew in his heart that it was well and truly done with him.

He heard a sniffle, and turned to see Layla and Devon, still held by the crows. Layla's anxious face slowly filled with relief.

'Are you good?' she said.

'Never been better,' said Robbie. 'Feet are a bit cold, though.'

Layla smiled, and Robbie smiled back. It was the most Robbie smile he had smiled in days.

'I *knew* you couldn't do it.'

Robbie turned back to Mother. The fear in her eyes had vanished completely. Now she was snarling. 'I *knew* you were too much of a snivelling little coward to finish the job— *What have you done to it?*'

It took Robbie a moment to realize she was talking about the Sceptre. He looked down at the silent rod in his hands, with its dull, lightless jewel.

Mother was shaking like a boiling kettle. 'You!' she spat. 'You . . . *broke* it? How did you *do* that?'

Robbie shrugged. 'By being good, I guess.'

'*You guess?*' hissed Mother, but her heart wasn't

in it. Her brows knitted tighter and tighter as she crawled to her feet and shuffled closer to the Sceptre. 'Where's its magic? I can't feel its magic!' Robbie could have sworn he heard her whimper. 'It's not *really* broken, is it?' she said pitifully.

Robbie breathed in. 'Only one way to find out.'

With every ounce of strength in his stick-thin arms, he dashed the Sceptre into the ground. The jewel shattered in a firework of green shards, which danced across the grey stone plain.

'*NOOOOOOOOOOOOOOOOOOO!!!*'

Mother fell to the ground again, and her body sagged. Robbie fought every instinct in his being to keep from comforting her. His heart was beating with a sickening force, and his hair was slicked to his face with sweat. He was shaking, and everything ached. But as he held the now jewel-less Sceptre, he had no regrets. Not one.

Slowly, Mother lifted her head, and Robbie winced. Her hair was even wilder than usual, her skin blotting with dark green spots; she was drained.

She took in a rasping breath, bared her teeth and hissed, 'You disgusting little worm. Do you have any idea what you've done?'

'A vague one,' said Robbie. Then he stood up as tall as he could. 'And stop calling me a worm. It's *rude*.'

'I know. I'm sorry—'

Robbie gasped as Mother's hands flew to her mouth. She peeled them away, horror-struck. 'I didn't mean that,' she said quickly. 'I didn't mean that at all. I'm *not* sorry. I'm *never* sorry! Now, are you all right— I DON'T CARE!'

Robbie looked at the half-shattered Sceptre in his hands. 'Ah,' he said. 'That's generations of evil power gone, isn't it?'

'No, no, no,' muttered Mother. 'Not this, *anything* but this . . .'

'Come on, Mother,' Robbie said softly, holding out his hand. 'I think you'd better get up and call your crows off my friends. Nice and easy . . .'

'IDIOT!' screeched Mother as she took Robbie's hand. 'I'll do what I please! Thank you for helping me up— *NO!*' She yanked her hand away and spun about the clifftop, her hands clasping strands of her oily black hair. 'What is this *feeling*?' she moaned. 'It's like a headache in my emotions.'

'Sounds like a conscience,' said Robbie. 'Now,

about the crows . . .'

Mother muttered irritably as she waved her hand, causing both crows to release their charges.

'ROBBIE!'

Robbie was nearly knocked off his feet as Layla flung herself into his arms. She stepped back, still gripping his shoulders.

'I really thought you were gone for a minute then!' she said with tears in her eyes. 'Just for a minute, though – I knew you'd pull through, obviously.'

Robbie grinned and hugged Layla again. Then he stepped back and, seeing Devon creeping up awkwardly beside him, caught her in a hug too. Judging by the way she blushed and stumbled once he'd let her go, Robbie got the impression that Devon wasn't quite used to hugs.

'Sorry, Devon,' he said. 'I should have asked first.'

'It's quite all right, young master,' said Devon breathlessly. 'But in all honesty I'd really like to be getting home now.'

'That sounds like a great idea,' said Robbie as he looked over the clifftops. 'But how exactly do we *do* that?'

'You can take my crows.'

Robbie, Layla and Devon all turned to Mother, who was now glaring at them sulkily from across the clifftop. She grimaced as she spoke. 'It's – ugh – it's the *least* I can do after all the kidnapping and attempted murder.' She retched, as though the words had left a particularly disgusting taste in her mouth.

Robbie blinked slowly. 'That's . . . that's awfully kind of you, Mother . . .'

'*Don't*,' snapped Mother, her arms crossed high against her chest. 'I don't want to talk about it.'

At her command the crows bowed and spread their wings, awaiting their new passengers. Layla frowned as Robbie beckoned Mother to approach.

'Well, we can't just leave her here,' said Robbie.

'I'm still not sure,' said Layla as Mother tried to glare her down. 'She's still very . . . glare-y.'

Robbie saw the ropes which had once bound Devon in a pile by his feet. He scooped them up, then shrugged awkwardly at Mother. 'If you would be so . . .'

Without a word Mother held out her hands, and Robbie tied her wrists together while trying his absolute best not to look her in the eyes.

'Is this enough to make everyone feel safe?' said Robbie to the others.

Layla turned to Devon. 'Up to you, Devon,' she said. 'You're the one she kidnapped – I think you should have final say.'

'I'd feel perfectly safe flying with her,' said Devon, before adding in a very small voice, 'If she gets into the sack, maybe.'

Robbie sighed, then picked up the sack Devon had been brought in and held it up to Mother. 'I'm awfully sorry about this, Mother, but for the sake of making everyone comfortable – and I *do* think you owe them, to be honest – would you mind climbing into this sack?'

CHAPTER TWENTY-FIVE

It hadn't occurred to Robbie how *small* the forest really was until he was soaring over it. A journey that had taken them days on foot was mere hours as they soared over the treetops, and it was only late afternoon when they finally arrived at the edge of the town. Robbie jumped off his crow, then helped Layla down too. The crows shook their wings wearily, and Robbie smiled up at the exhausted creatures.

'Thank you very much,' he said to the crows. 'We'll walk the rest of the way to give your wings a break. I'll make sure you get to rest for a week when we get back to the castle.'

The birds glanced at each other curiously before scrutinizing Robbie from the corners of their eyes, as though he were a bug that had done something unusual. Robbie tried to keep the nervousness out of his smile.

'Come on, Robbie,' said Layla. 'We've got one more passenger to disembark, remember?'

The two of them moved to Devon's crow and held out their arms.

'Right,' said Robbie. 'One, two, three . . .'

Devon pushed the sack from the crow, and Robbie's knees nearly buckled under its weight. Carefully, the two of them lowered the sack to the ground. Robbie untied the top and helped an extremely ruffled-looking Mother back to her feet.

'Sorry about that, Mother,' said Robbie, but she once again snatched her hand away and huffed.

'It's fine,' she said. 'I . . . *deserved* it.' She glanced away, trying desperately not to catch anyone's eye as her lip ever so slightly quivered.

'Right,' said Robbie. 'Let's get going, shall we?'

'We're walking through the town?' snapped Mother incredulously.

'The crows are too tired to carry us the rest of the way,' said Robbie.

'If the peasants see me with no guards they'll tear me to shreds!' Mother reached down and grabbed the sack, wriggling it over her head as quickly as she could with her hands still bound. Robbie glanced at Layla, who shrugged.

'Mother, what are you doing?' he asked wearily.

'I don't want to be recognized,' came Mother's muffled voice from within the sack. She was definitely unrecognizable; only her legs were visible, causing her to resemble a giant walking potato. 'One of you can lead me . . . if that's all right.'

'I'll do it,' sighed Devon, taking Mother's elbow as the four of them made their way towards Sinistevil Castle, crows hopping in tow.

Once they were back in civilization and trudging through the town, Robbie realized Mother had been right about the guards. There was something about the way people kept gasping when they saw him, or how shop doors suddenly slammed shut when he appeared at the window. His forehead grew moist with sweat. He tried to wipe it away with the back of his hand, but that was sweaty too.

By the time they'd reached the castle steps they'd amassed quite a gathering of townspeople behind them, all muttering the same words: '*A Sinistevil.*' Robbie tried his best to ignore them, his new heart pounding horribly as he once again fought the urge to throw up.

'You okay?' said Layla as they paused at the bottom of the steps.

Robbie sniffed. 'Not really,' he said in a small voice. 'I'm kind of . . . a little bit . . . absolutely terrified.' He looked back at Layla, trying to keep the wobble from his lip. 'I'm not *like* other Sinistevils, Layla. What if the servants don't trust me? Or the town doesn't like me? What am I supposed to do then?'

Layla smiled and patted his shoulder. 'Don't freak out,' she said. 'I'm right by your side, and I'm not going anywhere if I can help it—'

'*Over there! It's HIM!*'

Robbie felt a spray of spittle on the back of his neck. He turned around to see an old man, small and hunched, pointing a shaky finger right in Robbie's face.

'Um,' said Robbie. 'Hello.'

The old man's mottled pink face twitched with rage.

'*Hello?* I'll show you hello! Everyone, get over 'ere! It's one of 'em Sinistevil scum!' His yellowy eyes met Robbie's and his wrinkles contorted into a scowl. 'Brave, you are!' he spat. 'Coming out 'ere without any armed guards to keep us from kicking yer head in!'

'Why, thank you,' said Robbie nervously. He'd never spoken to a commoner before, aside from Layla. Maybe this was just how they greeted each other?

Robbie reached out a hand, but the old man staggered back, swatting it away. A muttering grew around them, and within moments the small crowd had grown even bigger, with everyone pointing and whispering at Robbie.

A pale-skinned woman gasped and pulled her children behind her. 'Stay back, children!' she cried. 'It's the Lord Sinistevil!'

The old man prodded Robbie in the back with his cane and Layla went to intercept him, but was distracted by two people who had pushed through the crowd: a tired-looking man in a muddy apron, and a woman with thick boots and gloves, and a face that Robbie found extremely familiar.

'Mum! Dad!' Layla cried as she ran to the couple, who embraced her tightly.

'Layla,' said her father, his voice thick with tears. 'You're safe!'

'Of course I'm safe,' sniffled Layla. However, when she tried to pull away they didn't let go.

'Keep back, love!' said her mother, holding Layla's arms as she tried to run to Robbie. 'He's dangerous! Thank the stars you got away from him!'

Robbie raised his hand to speak. 'No, I'm . . .' But Layla's dad stepped between them with his fists balled, and Robbie stumbled backwards as others joined him in an angry mob.

'We haven't eaten in weeks!' said a man, clutching his wife's hand. 'While *you* live in the lap of luxury!'

'The Queen had her armies tear down our houses because she was bored!' yelled a woman. 'Now we live on the street and it's all your fault!'

'Oh, no,' muttered Devon. Then, to Robbie's amazement, she sprinted away, her little legs flinging her up the castle steps before he could even call out to her. Mother wobbled as Devon disappeared, and for a moment Robbie worried that the people would wonder about her – but no one seemed at all bothered about the walking sack now that all eyes were on him.

Robbie didn't know what to do. The crowd had grown massively in a matter of seconds, and he could barely make out any words over the shouting. Several people were holding blunt objects in what he considered to be a very alarming manner. He searched frantically for Layla – there she was, being held back by her mother *and* father as she desperately tried to reach Robbie.

'Will you lot shut up?' she was shouting. 'He's not like her! He's not . . .'

But it was useless. Every word was drowned out by the yelling and jeering crowd now occupying the castle steps.

'We live in shacks!'

'We can't afford to feed ourselves!'

'We've had enough!'

'Grab him!' Robbie doubled over as the old man pulled him down by his shirt front. He pushed his withered old face into Robbie's and snarled, 'I'm sick of your mother's reign of hatred!'

'*SO AM I!*'

The crowd fell silent as Robbie's voice echoed across the castle steps.

The old man let go of Robbie's shirt and stumbled back in surprise. He was caught by a member of the angry mob, all of whom were now staring at Robbie in anxious silence.

Very slowly, Robbie stood up straight. He hadn't meant to shout so loudly; he didn't know he *could* shout so loudly. But something in him had snapped. He cleared his throat and addressed the mob.

'I'm sick of it too! I'm sick of the fact that my mother raised taxes so you can't eat. I'm sick of the fact that her army is tearing down your homes just because. And I'm sick of the fact that she doesn't seem to care about any of it! *I'm going to change things!*' He lowered his voice. 'Fingers crossed.'

The crowd began to murmur again, and a young woman stepped forward.

'You're a Sinistevil,' she shouted. 'Why should we believe that *you* have any sympathy for *us*?'

'Because . . .' Robbie clasped his hands to his chest and felt his heartbeat. 'Because I'm not evil. I'm not like the rest of my family – I'm not like Mother . . .'

'It's a Sinistevil trick,' said the old man, surging

forward once again. 'He wants us to let our guard down so we *think* he's good!'

The crowd nodded and murmured in agreement. Robbie swallowed as the old man continued.

'And then,' he hissed to the crowd, 'when our backs are turned, that's the moment that he'll—'

'*HE'S TELLING THE TRUTH!*'

Robbie leapt at the voice that cried out over the crowd. He looked around, wondering who it could possibly be. A frantically waving arm caught his eye, and there was Devon at the top of the castle steps – along with the entirety of the Sinistevil Castle staff. Robbie blinked up at the array of pristine red uniforms; there were guards, servants, a few of the cooks and one fairly raggedy-looking man weighed down by a heavy set of chains.

The man in chains put an encouraging hand on Devon's shoulder. 'It's true!' Devon cried. 'He's *not* evil!'

'And we should know!' shouted a chambermaid, straightening her apron. 'We've had to look after him for twelve years!'

The staff moved down the steps and merged with the crowd.

'One time at breakfast,' said one of the servants, 'I saw him accidentally swat a fly. He cried about it for days when he thought no one was looking!'

'The Queen once threw her dinner at him,' said a cook, holding a rolling pin above her flour-filled hair. 'Hit him right in the face, and what did he do? He sent compliments back to the kitchen!'

'He's never once shouted at any of us,' said a maid sheepishly. 'In fact, he once forgot to say "excuse me" when passing me in the corridor, and the next day I found a formal letter of apology at my station.'

'I caught him in the armoury once,' said a guard, wiping her knuckles on her breastplate. 'Trying on pieces of battle armour. Thought it was a bit worrying at first – thought he was planning a coup. Then he fell over cos it was too heavy, and I had to help him out of it.'

As one the crowd turned to Robbie, who was smiling proudly. He remembered that day. It had taken the guard fifteen minutes to help him back on to his feet. He cleared his throat.

'Why do you think Mother's never let me address you? Or lead her army? Why do you think she's been hiding me for so long?' He straightened up to his full height and lifted his chin. 'I make her look bad.'

The crowd seemed unsure, and Robbie felt his confidence dip. What else could he do to prove his absolute un-evil-ness? What more did these people want?

A loud gasp made him spin around. A townsperson had finally noticed the walking sack and decided to free the person within it. The white-faced boy was now being held up by two other townspeople, who were shaking equally hard.

'Oh, my goodness,' cried the boy. 'Is that . . .?'

The castle cook ran forward, then nearly fell back when she saw Mother, hands bound, hunched as small as she could possibly get. 'Devon was telling the truth!' the cook called. 'Robbie really *has* vanquished her!'

At once the muttering of the crowd grew louder and louder. Robbie waited until the clamour began to die down and they were once again quiet, all staring at him. He looked to Layla. Her parents were no longer holding her back. '*Keep going!*' she mouthed.

'I am here today,' he called across the crowd, 'as the new ruler of the Sinistevil empire. And as your ruler, I want you to know that I'm going to make a lot of changes. I'm going to need help, lots of help.' He glanced at Layla, who smiled widely. 'Because a lot needs to change. But I know I can do it. Because I, Robbie Sinistevil, am *not* evil, and I pledge to make sure that no person with so much as a hint of evil ever touches this throne again! Now, as the first decree of my reign over Waning, I order that . . . um . . . if someone could get me a pair of shoes, that would be very helpful.'

CHAPTER TWENTY-SIX

obbie sat on the edge of his four-poster bed and gazed out of the window. The sun was still beaming gloriously; in fact, it hadn't stopped shining the entire week he'd been home. This was perfect weather for the constant partying that had been going on throughout the streets of Waning, including Sinistevil Castle, since Robbie's return. The servants hadn't stopped smiling, something Robbie had never seen any of them do in his whole twelve years of existence. The world had changed.

And yet, Robbie didn't feel like he was quite keeping up with it. He peered through the window at the clear blue sky. It was perfect, because everything was perfect now – right?

Robbie sighed, then walked to the door and opened it a crack. He peered left and right down the hallway; no one around. Perfect. As silently as he could manage, he crept out of his room. 'One more normal breakfast,' he told himself as he slid round a corner. 'That's what I need. Just one more normal breakfast.'

He took his regular route to the dining hall, but he still couldn't shake the feeling of strangeness and unfamiliarity his new outfit brought – especially the shoes. He'd never managed to sneak about the castle so successfully before, or at least not without tripping over every ten minutes. But then again, he'd never worn clothes that *fitted* before.

He slipped through the portrait wing and came to a halt when he spied a familiar worn patch of carpet. Slowly, he turned to face what used to be his favourite portrait in the entire castle. As he looked up at the gloriously gory battle scene, realization began to bubble up inside him; he didn't even *like* the picture. It was too bloody, and no one in the picture seemed happy at all. His eyes found Brutus –

big, bold Brutus swinging the Sceptre, causing fear and destruction everywhere he went. Robbie's face twisted in embarrassment as he remembered that no more than a week ago, he'd been standing in this very spot wishing the person in the portrait was him.

'Sorry, Brutus,' he muttered. 'I don't think we're quite wired the same way.'

He took a step back and caught his full reflection in the glass, which lent a darker tinge to his green skin. His chest felt suddenly tight, and he quickly took off in the direction of the dining hall, not looking where he was going and crashing head first into . . .

'Devon!'

Robbie reached out to grab the little head servant as she fell backwards, but someone had already caught her, someone taller with the same mousey features as Devon, but hidden behind the biggest, bushiest beard Robbie had ever seen.

Devon's father set his daughter upright again, then his eyes widened as he recognized Robbie. 'Prince Robbie!' The man dipped into a bow before Robbie could protest, and Devon gave him a shy smile.

'Sorry, it's a force of habit for head servants,' she

said to Robbie. Then she noticed his outfit. 'Wow,' she gasped. 'Young master Robbie, you certainly look ready for your coronation today! How are you feel—'

'Thank you,' said Robbie quickly, waving the words away. 'That's very kind of you to say, but Devon – I thought I gave you the day off?'

'You did.' Devon nodded.

Robbie frowned. 'Then what are you doing here in the castle? In uniform?'

The corner of Devon's smile twitched ever so slightly. 'What do you mean?'

'I thought you'd want to be catching up with your father,' said Robbie, nodding politely to the bushy-bearded man.

'That's what I'm doing,' said Devon, gazing up at her father, who gazed back down at Devon as he wrapped an arm round her shoulder. 'It's wonderful, Robbie – now when I talk to him, he talks back!' She pointed enthusiastically at his mouth. 'See? No gag!'

'That's really lovely, Devon,' said Robbie, trying his best to keep up his smile. 'But surely on a day off you'd rather be . . . somewhere *other* than your place of work? Maybe in your own clothes?'

Devon's smile finally managed to slip from her

face. Her forehead creased as she glanced from Robbie to her father. When she spoke, it was barely above a whisper. 'I've not really had a day off before,' she said. 'I'm terribly sorry, young master Robbie, but I'm not entirely certain what one entails. What do I . . .' she gestured vaguely with her hand, '. . . *do*?'

'Well,' said Robbie slowly. 'What do you *enjoy* doing?'

Devon stared blankly, and for a horrible moment Robbie thought he'd broken her. Then her father squeezed her shoulder and chuckled.

'If I may speak, soon-to-be-King Robbie,' he said, and Robbie winced at the word *King*. 'The Queen left little time for leisure in the head servant itinerary. A whole day off is a real novelty for us!'

'What if I do it wrong?' whispered Devon.

'You'll have loads of chances to practise, Devon,' said Robbie. 'Now Mother's not in charge any more, I'll give you lots of days off!'

'Lots?' said Devon uncertainly.

'Yes! In fact,' Robbie threw up his hands. 'Why don't you take the whole *week* off?'

Devon's eyes grew huge and her chin slowly

dropped, like a fish realizing it was no longer in water. 'A *week* . . .'

'Maybe we should just start with the day,' said Devon's father. Then his eyes met Robbie's, and his smile fell. 'You've grown so big, young master. Devon's told me all about you, of course, and what you've been through. I can't help but feel responsible,' His eyes began to fill, and Robbie looked down at his shoes. Devon's father sniffed. 'I cannot offer enough apologies for my part in Queen Viella's plans, young master.'

'Oh, um,' said Robbie, fiddling with his sleeves. 'Well, you know . . . we all make mistakes. And Mother was quite overbearing, so I do understand . . .'

'I felt awful as soon as your heart was taken!' he went on, his beard growing soggy with tears. 'I wanted to tell you, as soon as you were old enough to understand, but when the Queen found out and threw me in the dungeon I could only imagine . . .'

'Really,' said Robbie, waving his hands. 'It's all right, I promise! It's all in the past now. Let's just start again!'

Devon's father shook his head. 'How you're a Sinistevil, I'll never understand.' He bowed low, then lifted his head and mouthed *Thank you*. He then slowly steered a still-unresponsive Devon by her shoulders and pushed her gently down the corridor.

Once they were out of sight, Robbie stopped smiling and ran the rest of the way to the dining hall, hoping with all his might that he wouldn't run into anyone else. The dining hall doors were in sight – and open! Robbie picked up speed, slid through the double doors and slammed them shut, leaning back against them as he tried to catch his breath.

The servants laying out breakfast turned and stared at him.

'Very sorry for running in like that,' said Robbie as he wiped the sweat from his brow. 'Would you mind awfully if I had breakfast alone today?' He stepped aside as the servants filed from the room. 'Thank you,' he said to each one as they beamed back at him. 'Thank you so much, I'm very sorry for the trouble …'

The doors clicked shut, and the room fell silent. Robbie sighed deeply, then shuffled to the table and grabbed a piece of toast from a rack. He made his way to his usual spot at the far end of the table, with a passing glance at the newspaper, which lay by the juice. He then fell wearily into his seat and lifted a slice of toast to his mouth.

'Still eating toast, I see.'

Robbie leapt up, the toast flying from his hand and landing halfway across the room. Mother stepped out from the shadows, glaring. 'I'd have thought a King would have graduated to more sophisticated breakfasts.'

Robbie gripped the back of his chair while he waited for his heart to stop thudding. 'Well, I've not actually been crowned yet,' he said. 'That's this afternoon.'

Mother narrowed her eyes. 'Oh, yes. How silly of me to forget.'

Robbie narrowed his eyes right back. 'Why are you lurking in the shadows, Mother?'

Mother's cheeks blushed deeper as she flashed her black teeth. 'You ran into the room looking terrified, and when you ordered everyone out I thought I'd stay behind and . . . and . . .' She growled a low growl, squeezing her eyes shut as though hit with a sudden headache, then forced the words through gritted teeth: '*Make sure you were all right.*'

Robbie let his shoulders drop. 'Your conscience still giving you bother, then?'

Mother crossed her arms as her lips curled into a snarl. 'I'd rather not talk about it, thank you.'

'I heard you complimented Layla on her tailoring the other day, she said you called her embroidery exquisite . . .'

'I said I'd rather not talk about it! Well? What's wrong with you? Why were you looking so nervous? Not that I *care*, of course.'

'Nothing's wrong,' Robbie lied. 'In fact, I'm having a lovely morning.'

'I said I don't *care*!' Mother attempted another sneer. Robbie raised his eyebrows, and she huffed. 'Fine. I'm *glad*, all right? I'm *glad* you're having a lovely morning.' She sighed. 'You've really had this "conscience" thing jabbering in your head your entire life? How do you cope?'

'You get used to it,' said Robbie with a shrug. For a moment neither of them spoke, until Robbie couldn't take the awkward silence any longer. Using his foot, he nudged a chair out from under the table and nodded to it. 'Join me for some toast?'

Mother tried to sneer, but her heart just wasn't in it. She glanced about the room before slowly edging towards the table. She didn't sit down, but instead put her taloned hands on the tablecloth and leant forwards, inching her nose closer and closer to the toast rack. She gave it a hesitant sniff. 'It doesn't look particularly substantial,' she said dubiously. 'How does this fill your stomach ready for a ride into battle?'

Robbie thought about this for a moment. 'I don't suppose it does, but I also don't think I'll be riding into battle any time soon, so it doesn't really matter. Go on, take a slice. I've got some jam here, if you want to make it look more like the blood of your enemies.'

Mother raised one eyebrow at Robbie. With her thumb and forefinger, she carefully plucked a piece of toast from the rack and held it to her lips. She took a cautious bite, and Robbie winced as her jagged teeth crunched. He counted the seconds as she chewed.

'Hm,' she said slowly. 'I suppose it's not *quite* as bad as I thought it would be.'

'I'm glad,' said Robbie. 'Tomorrow we can have orange juice.'

'Orange juice,' mused Mother, stroking her chin. Then she cleared her throat. 'I never thanked you for not letting me fall.'

'Oh,' said Robbie, fiddling with his sash as he tried to look anywhere but at Mother. 'Well, I wasn't going to let you die, so . . .'

'*I* would have let *you* fall, if it were the other way round.'

'Yes, I know.'

'Which isn't very *good* of me.'

Robbie looked up. Was that a hint of sadness he just saw flash across Mother's face?

'Well,' he said softly. 'Goodness is hard.'

'How sickly,' Mother grumbled as she rolled her eyes. She gnawed at her lip for a moment before she spoke again. 'I suppose you didn't turn out quite as worm-like as I thought.'

Robbie smiled. 'That's very kind of you to say, Mother.'

Mother grumbled. 'Thanks.'

There was a knock at the dining hall doors and Robbie called, 'Come in.'

Layla's head peered round the corner of the door frame, a wide grin spread across her face – until she saw Mother. 'Oh, sorry,' she said, shrinking back behind the door before mouthing to Robbie: *Do you need help?*

'I was just leaving,' said Mother, turning from the table. 'Good luck with your coronation, Robbie.' Mother's hand brushed the table discreetly as she shuffled from the room, and Robbie decided not to mention that he'd seen her snatch up the cartoons section of the newspaper.

Layla closed the door behind Mother and the grin sprang back to her face, the same grin she'd been grinning all week. (Robbie could tell from the creases on her cheeks.) 'One of the servants told me I'd find you here,' she said as she ran to the table and opened her arms. 'What do you think?'

Robbie took in her new purple uniform, complete with golden sash and epaulettes. He jumped to his feet and saluted. 'Layla Granite, you look positively regal.'

'It's not quite as sturdy as my overalls,' said Layla, hiding a blush. 'But I do believe my redesign is quite effective, don't you think? I look *incredible*. More than incredible,' she spun round and grabbed Robbie's shoulders. 'I look like I'm *in charge*!'

Robbie smiled at his friend. 'Layla, you look so in charge that if you told me to jump off the castle roof I'd do it. I've never seen someone look *more* in charge in my entire life!'

Layla's eyes widened at Robbie's outfit. 'Speak for yourself,' she breathed. 'I mean, your get-up was fancy before, but . . . whoa.'

Robbie frowned. 'I don't know why you're so surprised,' he said. 'You designed it.'

'Yes, but I've not seen it on you yet!' said Layla. 'It turned out . . . *wow*.'

A lot had happened in the madness following Mother's deposition, including a complete overhaul of Robbie's position in the castle. The royal tailors had decided it was high time he started wearing clothes that actually fitted, and were extremely happy that their new recruit just happened to be the person who knew him best.

Robbie had never worn anything that had only belonged to him before. Everything felt incredibly light after Brutus' clothes – he could run a mile in this cloak, which wouldn't snag, and these trousers, which wouldn't trip him up. Best of all were the shoes; at first glance the deep, deep purple boots had looked seven sizes too small, and Robbie wasn't convinced at all that they'd fit. But, just as Layla had promised, they were perfect.

Having a new wardrobe was amazing, but also thoroughly unnerving, because Robbie knew these clothes weren't just fancy for the sake of fancy. The vine-patterned black silk, the silver epaulettes and the crimson sash were all exceedingly regal because they weren't that of a hidden prince. They were the clothes of a King.

Robbie fingered the sash and glanced at Layla. 'Of course, I absolutely love it, but . . . do you think it's a bit much?'

Layla laughed. 'Obviously. But not for a coronation – they're *supposed* to be a bit much, that's how I designed them. Look, you don't need to worry about looking fancy all the time, I made sure the rest of your wardrobe is more of a regal-casual.'

Robbie's blush disappeared and, if it was possible, he turned greener.

'What's wrong?' said Layla. 'You're not having second thoughts, are you?'

'No, no,' said Robbie, wringing his hands and looking back at his abandoned toast. 'It's just . . .' He sighed. 'It's become very real, hasn't it?'

Layla nodded, then picked some lint from Robbie's shoulder. 'You know,' she said. 'When you first said you didn't want the Queen thrown in the dungeons I thought you were being a bit naive. She absolutely deserves it. However, and you know I hate to admit it . . .'

'What?' said Robbie.

The corner of Layla's mouth pulled into a bashful grin. 'I guess I was wrong, wasn't I? You never stooped to her level. You have this absolutely ridiculous way of seeing the good in rubbish situations, Robbie, and look what it's done – it's changing all of Waning. I might need to start taking this whole intense optimism thing seriously.'

'Being optimistic about Mother isn't going to fix all the harm she's done,' said Robbie glumly.

Layla nudged his shoulder. 'Well, obviously not,' she scoffed. 'But it's a pretty good place to start, right? That's what I think, at least. And if you managed to change *my* mind, I reckon that makes you pretty unstoppable!'

'Thanks, Layla,' said Robbie. He looked out of the window, at the multicoloured bunting which splashed the once-grey town with streams of rainbow. He put his hand on his chest and felt his heartbeat. He tried to smile as he looked back at

Layla, though it came out lopsided and unsure. 'I know this is what I've always wanted,' he said, a slight wobble to his voice. 'I'm ruling the kingdom, my mother's even proud of me ... It's just very different, is all. It's going to take a bit of getting used to.'

Layla took Robbie's arm and brought him right up to the window. In the reflection stood two people dressed as though they were about to rule the world.

'Well, I think that today is going to be the start of something incredible,' said Layla. 'And as your second-in-command ...'

'Actually,' said Robbie, pulling away. 'About that.'

Layla's smile quivered as she turned to Robbie. 'What?' she said. 'What's wrong?'

'Well, I've been thinking,' Robbie shrugged. 'You're already a royal tailor now. And to be honest, second-in-command doesn't seem like the best fit for you.'

Layla tried and failed to keep her lip from wobbling. 'Uh-huh?'

'No,' said Robbie, sighing. 'It sounds too "second fiddle" if you ask me. So, I was thinking something more along the lines of ... Head of Royal Advisors and Chief of the Department of Agriculture?'

Layla's eyes grew until her eyebrows nearly touched her hairline.

Robbie grinned. 'It's basically being my second-in-command but with a lot more power. You can get started with the royal advisors right away, they're very excited to hear your ideas. Waning won't know what hit it.'

'Can you do that?' gasped Layla.

'Um, duh, I'm King,' said Robbie. 'And I'm not just allowed –' he grabbed his sash and wrung it in his hands, '– I *need* you to. You've known me my whole life – let's face it, I'm helpless! I only found out Mother hated me *last week*. I'm twelve years old and can't even pick up on the social cues of a woman sending giant rats to chase me around a forest! I need as many people around to teach me as I can get.' Robbie's smile threatened to fall from his lips.

He looked up when he felt Layla's hands on his shoulders. 'All of those things are true,' she said.

'Thanks,' murmured Robbie.

'*But* . . . do you know one of the biggest signs of a strong person? It's when they don't let evil people blow out the spark of good inside them.' Robbie dropped his hands to his sides and let Layla readjust his sash. 'You stayed good, Robbie. That's what's going to make you an amazing ruler. And yes, we've got to work on all that other stuff, but that's what royal advisors are for.' She stepped back and smiled at Robbie. 'You're going to be an incredible ruler, Robbie Sinistevil.'

Robbie hugged his friend hard. 'And you're going to be an incredible Head of Royal Advisors and Chief of the Department of Agriculture.'

They stopped hugging and Robbie let Layla lead him to the door. 'Now, come on,' she said. 'You're going to be late for your own coronation.'

Robbie took one final glance at the blue sky outside the dining-room window. He knew in his heart that things were about to get a lot more difficult. In fact, he was certain that undoing all of Mother's evil was going to be a very long and very painful process.

But today was a good day. He could celebrate that.

Robbie smiled at Layla as they both opened the door and walked through it together.

THE END

ACKNOWLEDGEMENTS

As much as I'd love to take all the credit for this book, it was a huge army of supporters that made it happen. This list is in no way exhaustive, and I'm not being paid by the page so I won't list you all (but you know who you are). Special thanks to . . .

My family, who simply assumed I'd be an author at some point.

Margaret, Philip and all at LYMT, who were the first to convince me that my writing should be seen by other people (and who celebrated harder than anyone when it actually happened).

All at Brunel University but particularly Daljit, Max, Bernadine and Neil who assembled faster than the Avengers at my first panicked email about publishers.

Barry Cunningham and Kesia Lupo for their amazingly supportive welcome into the publishing community. Special thanks to my editor Kesia, who often knew Robbie better than I did and I'll always be grateful for that.

Sarat, for being my book dealer when I most

needed one.

Anne D, who was simultaneously elated and furious when I decided to leave North Wales to start 'writing properly'. All of Robbie's love and all of Layla's fire came from you.

THE LAST CHANCE HOTEL by NICKI THORNTON

Seth is the oppressed kitchen boy at the remote Last Chance Hotel, owned by the nasty Bunn family. His only friend is his black cat, Nightshade. But when a strange gathering of magicians arrives for dinner, kindly Dr Thallomius is poisoned by Seth's special dessert. A locked-room murder investigation ensues – and Seth is the main suspect.

The funny thing is, he's innocent . . . can he solve the mystery and clear his name, especially when magic's afoot?

'This mystery is a worthy prizewinner . . .
a jolly, atmospheric mystery.'
THE TIMES

'Hercule Poirot meets Harry Potter in this
mind-bending, magical, murder mystery.'
MISS CLEVELAND IS READING

Paperback, ISBN 978-1-911077-67-1, £6.99 • ebook, 978-1-911490-41-8, £6.99

TRY ANOTHER GREAT BOOK FROM CHICKEN HOUSE

THE MIDNIGHT HOUR by BENJAMIN READ & LAURA TRINDER

Emily's parents have vanished into the secret world of the Midnight Hour – a Victorian London frozen in time – home to magic and monsters. Emily must find them in the city of the Night Folk, armed only with a packed lunch, a stowaway hedgehog and her infamously big mouth. With bloodthirsty creatures on her tail, Emily has to discover the truth to rescue her parents. What family secret connects her to the Midnight Hour? And can she save both worlds before she runs out of sandwiches?

'Anarchic humour, rich imagination and poetic writing, interspersed with elegant line drawings, add up to pure delight — with a stowaway hedgehog as a bonus.
GUARDIAN

Paperback, ISBN 978-1-911490-90-6, £6.99 • ebook, ISBN 978-1-911490-91-3, £6.99

DEMELZA & THE SPECTRE DETECTORS
by HOLLY RIVERS

Demelza loves science – she loves it so much that she stays up late to work on her inventions. But she soon discovers she's also inherited a distinctly unscientific skill: Spectre Detecting.

Like her grandmother, she can summon the ghosts of the dead. When Grandma Maeve is kidnapped, Demelza and her pasty-faced best friend, Percy, must leap into action to solve the deadly mystery . . .

Talking skulls, family feuds, red herrings and a spirited (in every sense) heroine underpin this funny, fizzing debut . . .
DAILY MAIL

Paperback, ISBN 978-1-912626-03-8, £6.99 • ebook, ISBN 978-1-912626-82-3, £6.99

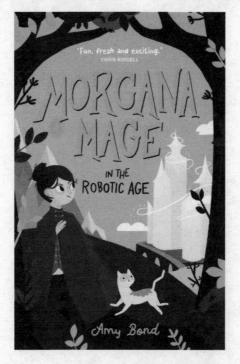

MORGANA MAGE IN THE ROBOTIC AGE
by AMY BOND

Morgana Mage loves robots, but as a witch she lives outside the nearby city with its shiny new technology. Science and magic are never mixed.

Determined to change things, Morgana finds a way into her chosen school of robotics, only to discover a secret that threatens both of her worlds.

It's up to Morgana to work out a solution – if she has the brains AND the spells to do it . . .

'Fun, fresh and exciting.'
CHRIS RIDDELL

Paperback, ISBN 978-1-912626-52-6, £6.99 • ebook, ISBN 978-1-913322-27-4, £6.99